STRUTTING LIGHTBUGS

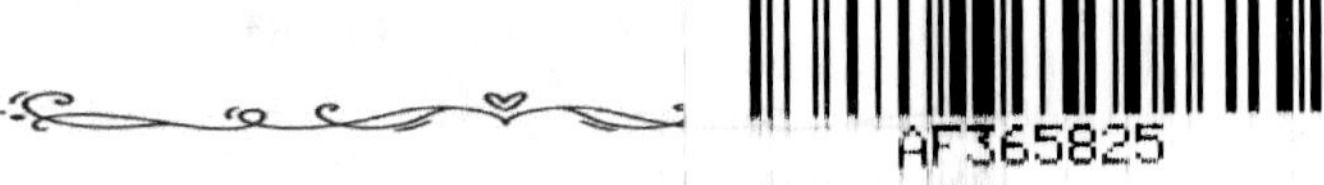

Kalam Babu
Lavanya Nukavarapu

eka
PUBLISHING

EKA PUBLISHERS
#118 Ushodaya Enclave, PO Miyapur
Hyderabad 500049 (India)
ekapresshyderabad@gmail.com +91 8008101590
www.ekapress.org

First Published in India by Eka Publishers 2021

ISBN: 978-81-949164-1-3
FICTION

Set in Sabon by Eka Publishers
Edited by Dr. Rizia Begum Laskar
Front cover painting by Uma Makala
Cover design by Abdul Rahman

Printed and bound in India by Eka Publishers

FOREWORD

'Strutting Lightbugs' is a genre-bender inasmuch as it addresses one of the most divisive, yet hyper-relevant, social issue of today, smartly wrapped in the foil of an ever-popular fiction trope – the supernatural thriller.

Kalam Babu and Lavanya Nukavarapu spin a riveting yarn that seamlessly fuses Indian culture, classical dance, spirituality, spirits, mythology, human psychology, history and most tellingly, gender boundaries and gender angst.

Their lucid storytelling and fluid style transport the reader into a mysterious, even sinister, world that moves seamlessly between the past and present. The protagonist, and with them the reader, are hurled into crises beyond the realms of normal human experience, yet somehow, magically, amidst all its breathlessness, the authors underline, and celebrate, the best facets of human behaviour, and the gender neutrality of art.

As a classical Indian dancer, I have, whilst plying my passion across the globe as a dancer, teacher and speaker, have very often encountered dancers whose biological gender, in their societies, have stigmatised their desire to dance – often irrevocably. The fact that it is not 'manly' for a man to have a desire to dance the dance forms traditionally associated with women, the fact that transgenders face ridicule for simply wanting to dance to the rhythms of normal life in their own manner, the fact that we bracket activities, vocations, sartorial sense into gender boxes based on man-made traditions and societal norms – are real, compelling issues. The human race has come a long way in terms of evolution, and the 21st century, and beyond, are perhaps the best period in our cumulative lives, to come to terms with, and blithely celebrate our diversity - to accept each other as we are, and want to be - not merely by how we look, what we wear, how we speak and how we 'must be' just because that's the way we 'should be.'

'Strutting Lightbugs' celebrates this ethos, this belief, and does so in a manner that engagingly entertains, yet effortlessly enlightens! I would go even as far as calling it a morality tale, and in the very best traditions of that genre, it is one that should well stand the test of time – past, present and future.

I wish Kalam and Lavanya every success with 'Strutting Lightbugs' and look forward to many more fabulous fables from them.

Sohini Roychowdhury

Dancer, Producer, Speaker
Founder – Sohinimoksha World Dance & Communications (Madrid-Kolkata-Berlin)
Founder – Sohinimoksha Artes de la India (Madrid)
www.sohinimoksha.com

PREFACE

Fiction invariably emanates from threads of reality. It can be based on a character in real life, an incident that has left a lasting impact on us, or a profound experience that shakes us to our core. This novel is an outcome of dipping into the first factor.

The interplay of a dancer with a supernatural force (and its motives) took us through gender roles and the medium of dance. It was an engrossing research that opened whole new vistas to us, which we were unaware of previously, through YouTube videos, podcasts, blogs, books and scholarly papers, a part of which we tried to capture and portray in the story. However, we make no claim to the accuracy and facticity of history/rituals or any other aspects of real world art. This work is, and will remain, a work of pure fiction.

There is no word 'lightbugs' in English. The Americans call fireflies as lightning bugs. We used lightbugs as the working title and the word stuck to us as more appealing and near to the story. Therefore, we went ahead with this word that we coined.

We are extremely grateful to Dr. Rizia Laskar who agreed to edit the book in a short span of time. Her inputs and feedback made the novel a fine polished piece. We also thank Uma Makala for agreeing to do the cover art; the image we had envisioned was depicted by her in a splendid painting, which is even better than our vision.

To educate ourselves on the vast field of the *devadasi* system and South Indian classical dance, we consulted the following books:

1. Nityasumangali: Devadasi Tradition in South India by Saskia C. Kersenboom

2. Given to the Goddess: South Indian Devadasis and the Sexuality of Religion by Lucinda Ramberg

3. Unfinished Gestures: Devadasis, Memory, and Modernity in South India by Davesh Soneji

We come from totally different backgrounds - gender, profession, academics and religion – this divergence, instead of pulling us apart, synergised our creativities into this first joint venture, which hopefully will pave way for more exciting stories from us going forward.

Kalam Babu

Lavanya Nukavarapu

18-Apr-2021

DEDICATION

We dedicate this book to all the artists out there, struggling against all odds pursuing their passions and making this world a beautiful place.

No matter what,
Always retain your light

Chapter - 1

Darkness was a few steps away, dusk had already creeped in.

The black stone of the wrecked fort stood in an eerie silence on a rocky hilltop. A huge boulder that looked like a giant resting its head on its arm greeted the visitors at the entrance. A skull with two crossed bones engraved on the boulder glared at the group of tourists who were busy clicking pictures of the ruins losing track of the day. There were weeds and wild shrubs all over the place adding a brown tinge to the blackish place. A tree with twisted and drooped branches, leafless and lifeless, covered the ground to the right of the fort and beyond it a vast expanse of woods with more boulders, shrubs and rocks waited impatiently for the night to close in. To the left of the fort was the pathway to the plains. Narrow and deep steps unwinded to the *kacha* road below which led to a *pucca* road which in turn led to a tar road and eventually to the main road.

A bus was parked just a few steps away from where the steps to the fort started. The driver of the bus wiped fresh sweat from his forehead. He grimaced as he saw the fort on the small hill and shouted into his mobile phone, "We have to leave. NOW!" He did not want to end up staying there one more minute. It wasn't dark yet, but the fort had already started to look sinister to him. And the twisted branches brushing one side of its walls felt like they would come to life at any moment.

Was it a flicker of light?

He rubbed his eyes and opened them wide. There were no lights. Just the black stone, the boulders, the black bark and the branches, a few shrubs, and the deep, stone steps that led to the fort. A hundred and fifty steps, he remembered. He had been there. Only once. They had arrived at the fort after wandering in the city for most of the day. And as it started to grow dark, his insides started to feel twisted as if someone was squeezing his stomach from within. He had never climbed the steps after that. He was always waiting down the hill at the entrance of the hike where the steps started. He swallowed a big lump in his throat, gasped for some air, and wiped the sweat off his face again, hoping for the group of students to hurry down the hill. Behind the minibus, there was a swish and flicker of lights in an uncanny pattern.

On the hill, one of the tourists in a red striped T-shirt, sitting next to the skull on the giant boulder, was gawking at the black of the closed shutter of his camera. His two best friends were busy smoking and arguing about whom to vote as their group's leader. They were standing under the black tree busy discussing under the cloud of their cigarette smoke. Others were busy clicking and trekking. A few of the pairs retreated behind the fort to kiss and smooch and he did not want to wander in that sort of imagination. A group of three girls were collecting some seeds, he looked at them and gave his best smile. He got three smiles in return - friendly smiles. He sighed.

The tourist in the red striped T-shirt, who was a college student, looked about his surroundings, the fort, the tree, the boulders, and precisely the boulder on which he was sitting. The skull caught his attention. Its eyes lighted in the dark, two yellow marbles of fire looking right through him. Shocked, he jumped from the rock and tripped but was able to balance himself. The two yellow marbles of fire flew from the skull into the night. *Fireflies!* He smiled. His stunned heart started to beat again. He opened the camera's shutter trying to catch the big fireflies that now rested on the bark of the black tree unnoticed by his friends who were still engrossed in their discussion. But before he could click, they flew away. Further into the woods, behind the black tree, he could see their flicker - on and off - teasing him, challenging him, beckoning him. He started walking in their direction, determined to catch them in his newly purchased DSLR. His friends were still arguing, they had hardly noticed him walk by them into the expanse.

A firefly droned over his head and landed on the leaf of a small tree whose branches hung low nearby. Another one followed and sat next to it. Shortly, a swarm had landed on that branch, giving the short tree a ghostly glare. As soon as he was about to click, the fireflies flew away, and he missed the shot. He had almost had it. He had even thought of a caption for his photo, "Strutting Lightbugs."

The flicker of the fireflies' light, the on and off nature of it captivated him. Hypnotised by the lightbugs, he kept walking in a trance, not knowing where he was going. He kept clicking and following them into the impending night. His walk crunched the dead grass under his foot. Nearby, a raven cawed at him. Somewhere, in the distance, an owl hooted. That did not make him aware that he was far away from civilization. And something lurked behind him, but he wasn't that lucid to sense the danger. His brain was numb. It was only reacting to the dance of the fireflies.

Suddenly, all the fireflies came together forming into a ball of light that rolled towards him, circled him and then formed into a huge tail and disappeared into the mouth of a dilapidated building.

A fort inside a fort?

He slowly walked towards this ruin unaware that he was entering into the mouth of the devil itself. Entering through the low height door, stooping all the way, he saw a dead shrub with thin branches and stems but no leaves, breathing in an eerie silence. It wasn't fully dark yet. At first, he thought it was his imagination. But as his ears adjusted to this new environment, he could clearly hear the rough breathing. It was as if there was someone around. But there was no one that his naked eye could see. In his camera flashlight, he could only see the dead shrub.

And shrubs don't breathe!
A sudden fear gripped him. He could not tell what exactly he was afraid of, but his gut told him there was something wrong about this place. His brain that was numb a few minutes ago now alarmed him to the danger he was in. He turned to walk out of the door but was halted by the sudden incoming gush of the fireflies. There were thousands of them. They came pouring in and settled on the thin leafless branches of the shrub. The dead shrub glowed in the evening light. The fireflies settled themselves in such a way that the shrub now looked as if it had glowing leaves. Tempted again, he opened the shutter of his camera to get a click of this glowing shrub.

Through the lens, he saw the fireflies slowly rising from the shrub in a coordinated movement as if someone was controlling them. The fireflies suddenly looked agitated. They formed once again into a ball, and like a raging comet advanced to him who now lowered his camera in a shock. Knowing what was going to happen, the photographer ran for his life. He came out of the ruined cave and was relieved to breathe fresh air, the eerie breathing was now gone. But there was a buzz. *The fireflies!* He started to run.

He had lost track of the path and time. He was not sure of how long he was running. Why did he even follow the damn fireflies in the first place? It was dark now. It was silent. No buzz, no breathing sound other than his own panting. He opened the camera shutter and looked at a 360-degree view through the lens. Out of nowhere, a raging comet of fireflies entered into his mouth; all of them, thousands of them. It was hardly ten seconds before the photographer fell flat on his face, dead. His insides charred, the exterior skin cold. The fireflies rushed out through his ears and nose, went and sat on the lone shrub in the cave that glowed violently in the dark. It had added the light and energy of a fresh soul.

Down below, the old engine puffed a cloud of smoke into the dusk that was growing darker by every minute. The bus moved, the driver felt relieved that they finally moved, unbeknownst to the group who were exhausted from the trek, one of their own was missing.

The driver took one good glance at the fort through his window before he sped into the village. The fort shone in the last remnants of the light as darkness started to engulf. A dozen hooded men, the driver called them watchers, protected the fort. The boulders turned into watchers at night. No one believed him when he said that. They scoffed at him and told him that they were just boulders, the arrangement of the small and big rocks gave them the appearance of hooded figures in the night. All those who scoffed at him should take a look at the fort now. He turned his gaze not intending to catch the attention of the watchers and sped away as darkness of the night replaced the dusk, and in that dark night, lights flickered on top of the hill, in the fort and in the deep cave behind the fort.

Not very far away from the devil's lair, a temple carved in black stone sprawled across several acres, spanning several centuries. If the fort was a tourist attraction, the temple did better. It was not only a tourist attraction but also an architectural wonder. Not to mention that it was a devotional bank where devotees not only deposited their devotion but also their artwork. It had one of the most beautiful daises in the world. And an atrium that put every other grandeur hall to shame.

The main deity is Lord Natraja[1]. A big sculpture almost the height of an average man stood at the entrance of the main temple carved in black stone and greeted the devotees. Lord Natraja in one of the Natya Shastra[2] poses, the right hand in *abhaya mudra*[3], and the left hand in *dandahasta mudra*[4], his one leg lifted in the air and the other leg crushing a demon, his face serene, eyes closed, a mark of the third eye on his forehead, his wild tresses scattered in the air and forming a fan behind him.

This evening a large *diya* made of stone is lit in front of him. It had small slots for mini *diyas* - a total of 108 *diyas* in one big *diya*. There are two bronze tall *diyas* placed on either side of the statue. A beautiful *rangoli* is drawn in front of the deity. There are flowers spread on the leg that is fixated to the ground. A garland of fresh lotus flowers adorned his bare chest. The scent of sandalwood mixed with the incense lingered in the evening air.

A long and wide corridor with carved pillars led to the main temple. Each pillar sculpted beautifully and exquisitely with dancers in different art forms. These dancers were poised in different *mudras*. It was rumoured that long ago the first king who ruled this land was so madly and deeply in love with one of his *Narthakis*[5], that he had the sculpture sculpt her in different dance poses. It was also said the king himself was so fond of dancing that he secretly learnt from his courtesan and he performed the art form in his private chambers in front of Lord Nataraja (idol). The king's teacher and his mistress were his only audience. And, if you, as a tourist, had a keen eye, you would recognise him in the midst of these dancing sculptures, a man in love with dance. In those old days' men who danced were considered as an embarrassment. It was a women's forte. And for a king to be practising this

---

[1] Hindu God Shiva as the divine dancer
[2] The Sanskrit treatise on performing arts.
[3] A hand gesture of fearlessness.
[4] A hand gesture.
[5] A courtesan.

art form, would have become a laughingstock to his subjects. He would have easily been overthrown by his own army. Rules that were made long ago by men who worshipped the dancing lord, the God of all gods, considered and treated men who danced as impotent.

The winds of time buried the names of the *raja*, the *narthaki,* and the *shilpi*[6] under the rocks of the temple but gave wings to the story.

In the heart of the temple, there is a podium for *pravachanam*[7], *bhajans*, *harikathas*, *kirtanas*[8], and small dance programs. But the main attraction is the *mandapam* outside the temple. Carved out from a single black boulder in concentric circles, it also served as steps to reach the eighth circle on the top. The topmost circle also served as the stage which had a big circle in dull white and shining silver paint embodied with geometrical and symmetrical drawings. When you see it from the side or standing near to it, it looks like Mandala art with no particular form or design or image, just an intricate design in a circle. But if you were to climb the small rocky hills inside the temple campus surrounding the podium on one side, and view it from an elevated angle, the geometric design would become an *Ardhanareeswara*[9]. The concentric circles of the stage portrayed paintings of musical instruments, the ragas and ancient Sanskrit slokas in Telugu script on them. There were two statues of Nataraja across the podium facing each other in *Tandava Natya*[10] poses.

Again, the painter was unknown, but her story was known - she had painted the king and the *narthaki* together in one form, the design opposed by several priests who eventually agreed that it was the painting of the *Mohini Avataram*[11] in a dancing pose. Whatever the story was, whoever painted the fabulous art, the temple was famous for this stage, pure and sacred for many dancers who dreamt of dancing on the stage, and while dancing on that stage felt close to the divine energy himself.

---

[6] Sculptor.
[7] An explanation of spiritual idea or doctrine or treatise in Hinduism
[8] Narrating, reciting, telling, describing of an idea or story in Indian religions.
[9] A composite form of the Hindu deities Shiva and Parvati (the latter being known as Devi, Shakti and Uma).
[10] Tandave Natya is the divine dance of Hindu gods.
[11] A Hindu Goddess and the only incarnation of Vishnu in female form.

That evening, the temple was decorated in lights for the *Kuchipudi* dance performances that were to be held shortly. *Diyas* were lit, the *gopuram* was decorated with colourful lights. Petromax lights were installed in the temple campus. The event started with the compère introducing the programme and extending a warm welcome to the audience. The first performance was *Ganesh Stuti*[12], followed by a chapter from *Sundarakanda*[13]. The third performance was based on *Mohini Avataram* - Lord Vishnu stealing the *amrutha*[14] from demons and giving it away to gods.

The dancer walked gracefully onto the stage and did her *Namaskaram*[15]. The live music troupe started the music. A low tune of violin filled the air. The lights dulled, dispersing a reddish orange hue on the stage highlighting the dancer on the center stage poised as *Mohini*. Draped in white and red, her eyebrows arched up and down beautifully followed by the movement of the eyes, and then the flow of her hands in different *mudras*.

Her hips swayed to the *tabla*, her alta adorned feet in *ghungroo* jumped and swirled in the air gracefully as if the dancer did not have any weight. The dancer magnetised the audience with her charming looks, delicate expressions, and captivating dance movements. Neither in the audience nor the fellow dancers had seen such poise, such grace, and such smooth flow of movements. They were all in awe. They were hypnotised by the dance like the demons would have been hypnotised by the beauty of *Mohini* and handed her the pot of *amrutha*. No one wanted to blink their eyes and not see the beauty in front of their eyes even for one fraction of a second.

There were photographs being clicked continuously, a video reel ran continuously capturing the entire dance event. And when the dance ended, there was a huge applause, the sound of which echoed in the evening for a minute long. No one wanted the dance programme to end. They wanted *Mohini* to dance forever. But like all good things come to end quickly the dance performance also ended. The dancer bowed gracefully, did her *Namaskaram*, and left the dais. And as the dancer left, the compère announced the name of the dancer.

---

[12] Praising Lord Ganesha through a song or verse.
[13] A chapter in Ramayana on Hanuman's journey to Lanka
[14] Ambrosia in Sanskrit.
[15] A dance salutation/prayer before and after the dance.

Kiranmayi held her breath for a brief moment and breathed out a relaxed sigh. She was stunned at the audience's reaction. A drop of tear slid through her right eye, smudging the *kohl* slightly. Her lips trembled with happiness; her ears enjoyed the sound of applause. As she walked down the stage, she could see a few dancers, the organisers, and the compère nodding at her in admiration. She smiled at all of them gracefully not uttering a single word. She did not expect such great love from the audience. It was all overwhelming, and there was a lump in her throat. She knew that as soon as she would enter the green room, she would cry. This evening would be one of the greatest memories of her life, a memory she would cherish forever and visit again and again whenever she wanted courage and inspiration. Kiranmayi walked briskly and gracefully to the green room at the back of the temple. At that very moment, a swarm of fireflies swirled around the temple's *gopuram*[16] in raw rage.

---

[16] A large pyramidal tower over an entrance gate to the temple precinct.

Chapter - 2

The greyness was evaporating slowly. At least, that's what Kiran thought.

The bright orange of the dawn filled his room already but, in his mind, it was still grey, a shade brighter than before but still grey. The orange appeared still dull to him, a shade better but still dull. It was the start of a new day. He felt good today. He woke up with a smile on his lips which was not very frequent. No classical music today. He switched on to English music on the FM and marched into the bathroom leaving the door ajar to hear the music as he freshened up and got ready for the office. Michael Jackson screamed black and white from the radio as the tap creaked and water rushed into Kiran's palms.

A routine he followed diligently, whether his heart was in it or not. 9 - 5 office regime, that's what he called it, and he stuck to it. Not a second more, not a second less. He was never late, he never left early. But he was good at consuming the leaves allotted to him. He did not believe in overtime or compensatory leaves. He arrived at 9 am and left at 5 pm daily. He did not care about office politics or rumours. Nor did he flirt with girls. He was formal to everyone even if they were not his boss. Except Ravi. He had tried to keep Ravi too within that office circle, but Ravi seeped into his system. He was Kiran's only friend both at work and outside work. It wasn't Kiran's fault at all. He used the same rules that he followed for keeping distance between him and people, especially at work. But the problem with Ravi was, that he had a poking nose, and he did not understand borders. This was definitely not the reason that he was able to transcend the social circle drawn by Kiran, but more so because of his selfless heart which was a rare ingredient in human commodity.

Kiran smiled at his friend who was seriously browsing on his latest mobile, sitting on his motorbike parked in the parking area. It was 8 am Ravi always waited for him. While Kiran believed in 9 to 5, Ravi was one of those guys who came early and left late. Not that he was dedicated to work but, he was a serious candidate for the office political parties and for the upkeep and running of rumours section. From the parking area to the accounts section, Ravi would fill in Kiran with all the news, gossip, sports updates and bad jokes which never incited a smile in Kiran. But Ravi was a "I-don't-give-up-that-easy" type of guy so he started using a lot of creativity these past few days only to annoy Kiran more. Today, however, was an exception as for almost one minute Ravi was silent as they walked together.

"You did not speak for one whole minute? You earn a coffee from me today," Kiran patted his friend's shoulder.

"And breakfast?" Ravi asked.

"For that you have to keep calm until 9," Kiran placed his arm on his friend's shoulder.

"No. I will buy breakfast for the two of us like I always do but I can't stay without talking." Ravi showed his phone's picture gallery to Kiran. There were photos of a dancer in different poses.

Kiran sighed. "Why don't you leave the dancer alone?" Kiran removed his arm and increased his pace.

"Why should I?" Ravi tried to catch up with his friend's pace. "You should have seen her performance yesterday. Mind-blowing. Words fall short to describe her beauty."

Kiran kept walking not reacting at all to his friend's comments. But this did not discourage Ravi. On the contrary it fuelled him to talk more and more about the dancer.

When they reached the canteen, Kiran gave the tokens at the counter and collected the breakfast plates. Ravi was still pouring praises for the dancer. Kiran tore a piece from the *idli*, dabbed it generously in the chutney bowl and chewed on it praying silently for his friend to stop. But his friend did not fall silent even when he gobbled the *idli* and the *vada* pieces, speaking with his mouth full which only irritated Kiran more. He listened till at one point he could bear no more and became furious. He was blowing on the hot spoonful of *sambhar* and instead of putting it into his mouth, he shoved it back into the bowl.

Crossing his arms, he questioned Ravi, "What has anything to do with the type of dance? Any dance form is art, and no dance is superior to the other. Just because we are Telugu does not mean *Kuchipudi* is superior. And just because we are Indians also does not mean that our dance forms are the greatest. Do you know ballet requires years of focus and training?"

"I don't know all that. Ours is the best. And after seeing yesterday's dance performance, I am fully convinced that it is the woman's charm and her grace that makes it beautiful and mesmerizing. Tell me, can ever a man ever dance like a woman? It is not possible. And if he dances like that, then he is not a…" Ravi winked trying to emphasise what he was stating which was very clear to Kiran. The winking was not at all required.

"What nonsense!" Kiran's raised his voice a little, displaying his dissatisfaction at his best friend's thinking. "Then according to you, men should not dance at all."

"They should. But not graceful dances like *Bharatanatyam* and *Kuchipudi* or *Kathak*. I think *Kathakali* or hip hop that you do sometimes." Ravi drank the *sambhar* from his bowl and gave a satisfied burp. One of the helpers in the canteen placed two cups of coffee on their table and left collecting the plate that Ravi emptied just now.

"Do you even know that *Kuchipudi* was founded by a male and when it originated it was performed by an all-men troupe. For several years, it was men who practised and popularised it. And have you forgotten the name of Guru Dr. Vempati Chinna Satyam and his contribution to *Kuchipudi*?" Kiran took a big bite off a big piece of *idli*, chewing it slowly and glaring at Ravi who did not seem convinced at all.

"All that is okay. But tell me this? If there is a woman dancer on one stage and just right to this stage, say there is another stage and a male dancer is performing exactly the same dance that the female dancer is performing, tell me honestly, which performance will you watch? The man's or the woman's performance?" Ravi sipped the hot coffee waiting for his friend's reply.

"Whoever dances the best. And not because it is performed by a man or a woman," Kiran replied, stuffing the last piece of *idli* into his mouth. His *sambhar* was left untouched. But he did not bother to drink it. He just left it there for the canteen helper to pick it up.

"You are not being honest. I for one would watch the female dancer. And this answer would be the majority's voice."

Kiran shrugged.

"Are you drinking it?" Ravi asked.

Kiran shook his head, and Ravi emptied the small *sambhar* bowl gulping it all in a second.

"If you would give prominence to a female dancer just because she is beautiful or simply female, then you are degrading art and you are sectionalizing it as one gender's monopoly."

Kiran blurted out pushing aside the empty plate and the *sambhar* bowl that Ravi had just emptied.

"All I am saying is that a woman's grace and beauty adds to the beauty of dance especially the traditional classical dances," Ravi argued.

"And men cannot be graceful?" Kiran snapped.

Ravi laughed. "You know what they call men who are as graceful as women?"

"I never imagined that you were so judgemental and gender biased," Kiran ended the discussion.

This time Ravi shrugged. And Kiran shook his head in dismay. He then said very slowly, leaning over the table to his friend, "Today is the last date for paying the fees for the second semester of MBA."

"I forgot!" Ravi almost screamed.

"I paid yours as well as mine, yesterday itself," Kiran leaned back. Ravi grinned.

He was late by 10 minutes because of their discussion on dancing. And he hated that. Kiran followed a strict office regime. Though he was late today, he was the first to arrive. Even his boss, the Accounts Manager has not arrived yet. He settled in his chair and started going through the vouchers that he had pinned on Friday on his table. He switched on his computer and started going through the vouchers planning to record them first. Mr. Sarma, the Senior Accountant arrived followed by the manager, Ashok Kumar. Kaushalya, a Junior Accountant as usual, was the last. The other team member, Shashi Priya, was on maternity leave and most of her work was distributed among all three of them which Kiran happily took up but Kaushalya and Sarma Sir kept complaining and tried to shift their part of work to Kiran. But Kiran was smart enough to reject it and he had made it very clear to all of them that he was not in favour of overtime even though the company gave him overtime allowance. Sarma Sir and Kaushalya were angry with Kiran and showed their anger in tantrums and taunts but Kiran did not budge.

He was liked by his boss Ashok Kumar who was fine with Kiran not doing overtime. He was happy that he was saving cost for the company. And when Sarma Sir and Kaushalya would complain about Kiran leaving sharply at 5 pm and they staying back and clearing the backlog, Ashok would smile and simply ignore them. It was slightly more than a year that Kiran joined "Super Motors and Automobiles," and Ashok was very happy with him. Kiran not only learned the job fast, but he also automated a few manual things saving everyone's time. The boy had a future, and he had already recommended a good pay hike and a fat bonus for this year. Ravi worked in the dispatch department. He was responsible for maintaining inventory of the automobile parts and other motor parts manufactured at the factory and for accounting of the stock and dispatching the goods and maintaining the sales memos and other related stuff of the inventory parts. He too reported to Ashok Kumar who was the accounts manager for all the smaller departments within Accounts which included Costing, Accounts, Payroll, and Sales.

It was almost 11 am. Kiran collected all the vouchers which required his Boss's signature and was about to knock on his door when Ravi opened the door with a loud thud announcing, "Have you all seen the news? There is a murder. Police found a body this morning on the fort's premises."

All of them started to speak at once, even the office assistant Ramalingam who had just brought tea for everyone. Sensing that something was wrong, Ashok came out of his cabin and he too joined the discussion. Ravi was showing them some YouTube video covering the news of the murder.

"I thought our small town was safe," Kaushalya sighed.

"How can you say it is murder, it could be an accident as well. The video just tells that they found a body," Sarma Sir commented, rubbing his glasses.

"But how did the group miss one of their boys?" Ashok remarked, scratching the bald spot on his head.

Kiran tried to interrupt, asking Ashok to sign the vouchers so that he could file them. He was more concerned about his work, and he did not want a pile of vouchers lying on his worktable just because his boss did not approve them on time. He hated unwanted papers scattered on his desk. He could not concentrate. He kept his desk organised and neat. Everything had a place on his desk, every paper had to go in a file which in turn would occupy a spot in a cabinet or a shelf. But Ashok was not listening to him. He was busy discussing the murder with the other staff members. A few team members from Costing and Sales were also there and everyone discussed the body and the police interviews.

"Yes Sir, that is strange. How can they forget one of their team members on the fort?" someone from the Costing department commented.

"They realised this morning that one of them never boarded the return trip. They called the police and after a detailed search they found him, but not alive," Ravi dramatised the entire event.

"This is horrible." A female voice made its way in between the male voices.

Kiran stood with the vouchers in his hand to get a signature, but everyone was engrossed in discussing the murder. Work could wait. It is not every day that someone gets murdered.

"Fresh update on the TV. It seems they are showing on the Telugu news channel," Ramalingam announced.

Everyone fled out of the room to watch the TV in the canteen to know fresh updates including Ashok. Ramalingam quickly cleared the cups and he too left the accounts cabin. Kiran let out a heavy frustrated grunt. The vouchers had to wait.

It was lunch time. Kiran collected his lunch plate while giving the lunch token at the counter and settled next to Sarma Sir in the canteen. Kaushalya was sitting opposite to them talking on the phone with her mother. Ravi was nowhere to be seen. But Kiran did not wait for him to join. On the television, there was a ticker scrolling continuously about the murder. The news anchor dressed up in her best *sari* and tons of makeup on her face sensationalised the murder with all the jargon she had learnt in her journalism class. She also requested everyone to be careful as a cold-blooded murderer was on the loose.

Kiran did not want to look at the news reader. So he looked down at his plate, mixed the curry with a small portion of rice, all the time thinking about the unsigned vouchers on his desk. Ashok had left for a meeting and he will be back only by 4 pm. The curry was sour, too much tamarind, he said to himself. He chewed forcibly gulping water all the while listening to the news anchor in gaudy makeup. He need not look at her. But he can at least hear her. "Our correspondent, Vijay Babu, is right outside the office of the Medical Examiner where the autopsy would be conducted shortly."

The screen flashed over to Vijay Babu, and Kiran lifted his face relieved to watch some other face. Vijay Babu talked into the mike giving the updates, "The autopsy has not yet started but I was able to talk to the medical examiner for a short period of time and his preliminary inspection of the body revealed no exterior wounds on the skin. The dead subject, Prakash Karnur, fell face first on the ground with his mouth and eyes wide open, his nose showed injury from the fall, but his oesophagus was burnt and charred. A detailed autopsy would prove the cause of the death as to why his throat was burned." And then Vijay went on giving the minute details of the dead body, how his eyes were wide open as if he had seen the biggest horror of his life.

Kiran could no longer take it. This was the hour of music. They played either Telugu songs or classical music and sometimes cricket when it was cricket season. But today, it was about death and its gory details. He switched on music on his mobile phone and plugged the earphones into his ears. He slowly pushed the sour curry to Sarma Sir who would not only eat anything and everything but also digest it easily by letting out a burp. Kiran's stomach was as sensitive as his mind, and it too followed a strict regime.

He loved the canteen's *rasam*. He tasted a little, clicked his tongue in satisfaction and poured the *rasam* from the bowl into the rice. He crunched the *papad* from the side and pushed it inside his mouth with the spoon of the hot *rasam* rice. The hot and spicy *rasam* felt great on his tongue, at last satisfied with the lunch he had been eating. He looked up at the screen and stopped chewing immediately. His eyes stopped blinking. They were fixated on the woman speaking into the mike.

She was wearing a red *sari* embroidered in light golden *zari*. The gold *buttalu* (type of earrings) with small red beads kissed her cheeks as she talked with vivacious energy. A big red *bindi* adored her white forehead. Her eyebrows were perfectly arched and pitch black against her fair face. Her eyes, big and round, were full of life. For one moment, Kiran thought she was speaking to him directly. He removed the ear plugs and her sweet but angry voice filled his ears.

She was pleading with the police department to catch the murderer and justice be served. "Our town is a safe tourist spot. We are known for our architectural wonders and our culture. And it is our prime responsibility to assure the world that this was a one-off case. An unfortunate incident. We must bring justice to the boy and his parents. This matter should be expedited quickly by the police and given high importance." She then folded her hands and said thank you.

Kiran was so lost in watching her that he did not realise Sarma Sir taking half of his *papad* from his plate and scooping half of the sweet as well. But he was not bothered about the *papad* or the sweet. His stomach was full. His heart was full. It got all the required nourishment and nutrition from the woman in the red *sari*, at the mere sight of her. He was transported to some other world, some other dream world where the woman from the TV channel was speaking to him.

He did not understand what she was telling him in that dream world, but it felt like a song the lyrics of which he sang before, but he could not remember now. He had lost them in the lanes of his puberty, where he became a man from a teenager. The words lingered at the back of his mind, but he was too busy growing up, completing his studies and making a career, that he completely forgot about them. And now as the song played, the lyrics at the back of his mind suddenly made sense to him. He was trying to find the first word when the woman on the TV was gone. Replaced by the heavily made-up woman who irritated him. He sighed.

He tried the next spoon of *rasam* rice, but he couldn't. He left the half-eaten rice and walked away. Sarma Sir happily took the *papad* and the untouched sweet from Kiran's plate. And as Kiran walked, he heard the news anchor say, "That was Sravanya Mullapudi, the renowned dancer of *Kuchipudi*…"

He walked back in a trance to the Accounts department. As he opened the door, the afternoon sun rays peeped through the window spraying a light orange shade. The leaves of the mango tree, its branches overgrown, brushed the windowpane masking some of the sunlight. The day wasn't black or white, it wasn't even grey. He did not know what to call it. Today was different from all the days. He did not expect that a mere look at her would have such a strong effect on him. All these years he had not forgotten her. He did not make an attempt to meet her or talk to her. Because he knew she would not entertain him. She would not talk to him or agree to meet him. He knew he would never reach up to her level in terms of family or financial status. Neither would she come down to his level where she would see the real him, see his passion, see his art, see his greyness. She was like the rest of the world; she would only see him in either black or white.

He then wondered, walking slowly to his chair, what was the shade of love, anyway? Black? White? Nope. A thousand shades of grey, each shade darker, deeper. Or was it pure orange, the light of a million fireflies glowing in unison in his heart?

He sank into his chair lost in the greyness of his mind.

Chapter - 3

That night Kiran switched on the TV when he was back home in the hope that one of the TV channels would replay Sravanya's interview. He browsed impatiently but none of them showed what he wanted to see. One of the channels was showing the dance performance of Kiranmayi, the dancer Ravi was talking about in the morning. Not her full dance but shots of her dance performance along with other dance performances on that day.

As a voiceover, a male newsreader was drawing parallels to the dance performance and the killing that happened on the fort. While everyone was celebrating life and art at the temple, some unknown dark force had stepped into the shadows performing its own macabre dance. Kiran felt that the newsperson was bad at metaphors.

He switched to another channel where the medical examiner was being interviewed. He was an old, skinny man with a lot of hair in his ears and half bald with brooding and puffy eyes. The man appeared to Kiran as dead as the carcasses he examined. He was talking in a very boring voice, "I have never seen such a thing. The throat was burnt, half of the stomach was burnt and the rest half charred. But the skin was not affected. It didn't even turn black. It was intact."

"What might be the reason?" The journalist asked.

The medical examiner fell silent for a brief second, his eyes pointing to the sky lost in some deep thought and before he opened his lips to speak in that dull voice of his, Kiran changed the channel. Disappointed, he switched off the TV and tried to sleep.

As he began to drift away, outside his window, lights went on and off in a steady hypnotizing rhythm. He did not notice them. His eyes were half closed. He was drifting into a state of dreams where he was walking in a strange place. It was dark. There was a shimmer of light - on and off. Now it was there, now it had disappeared. He kept walking to the turning on and the turning out of the lights. The fireflies were calling him. They formed into a beautiful face, the face of Sravanya. She smiled at him. As he went near her trying to hold her face in his palms, she vanished and a thousand fireflies flew away from his palms flickering on and off, radiating the most beautiful light he had ever seen.

Not very far away, just a few houses away, a few fireflies had entered through the window into a house. The wife was asleep in the bedroom. The husband was watching the interview of the medical examiner on the TV and thinking about the various possibilities. The theories given by the medical examiner were absurd. In the midst of the TV voice, he heard a swish.

He ignored it at first. There was again a low buzz. He stood up and checked the room. The buzz was more prominent now. A bee must have come through the window. He took a magazine determined to shoo away the bee. The buzz was irritating him. Suddenly, it stopped. He went back to the sofa watching the news. The buzz was back. It was now close to his ears. Something droned past him. But he could not see what it was. He took the magazine and hunted for the bee that had disturbed his peace.

He was happy that his wife was asleep, and he could enjoy some calm. And now this stupid bee had to ruin his peace. Why can't he watch the news peacefully in his own house? He reduced the TV volume so that he can focus on the sound of the buzz, to determine its location and then drive it out. Or he will simply kill it with a hard blow from the magazine. The buzzing sound was coming from the floor, from underneath the sofa. He bent to look under the sofa, he saw lights flickering under the sofa in a strange pattern.

What the hell?

And suddenly, like a dragon's tail, the lights snaked from beneath the sofa and over his shoulder and out of the window. *They were gone?*

Not so easily. He heaved a sigh of relief but the buzz was back again. More violent and louder. It started to sound like tinnitus. He shut his ears tightly and closed his eyes. And when he opened his eyes after a few seconds and removed the hands over his ears, the lights of the room went off.

Power cut?

And in the darkness, a spot of light flickered on the TV. Another spot. Then another. The spots became a blob and slowly it covered the entire TV with a uniform switching on and off like a torch light. His eyes blinked in rhythm to the off and on of a thousand spots of light. As if they were talking to him, a voice in his head asked him to turn around, open the door and walk out into the night. He crossed many houses walking in a trance, he saw the flickering of lights in a distance. He followed them. Soon he was on a tar road and on a *pucca* road and finally on a *kacha* road.

He kept walking. He reached the steps of the fort, he started to climb, one by one, in a sleep-walking state. As he reached the top, the watchers glared at him through the hoodies, the skull on the giant boulder glowed in the dark, the dead tree watched him with a mocking smile. As he crossed the tree, he bumped on its bark and came to his senses.

What am I doing here?

The last thing he remembered was watching news on the TV. The ghostly buzz was back. He could hear it. His hands started to shiver, his legs trembled. He was not sure what he was looking at. He ran for the steps. But he slipped and fell down. He tumbled and rolled over the steps hurting himself. He was halted by the shrubs.

He took a deep breath and as he was trying to get up, a swarm of angry fireflies appeared suddenly from nowhere trying to enter into his mouth. In a shock, he fell and rolled over the steps again halted by the dead weeds, but this time dead from the fall.

His face was frozen with an expression of terror stuck on to his face, blood from the wounds of the fall slowly covering his face and eyes. The swarm of fireflies watching from a few yards away vanished into the night.

The fort and its boulders stood in eerie silence as the only witness to a cold-blooded murder waiting for the mysteries of the night to unravel.

A new day. Kiran woke up to the alarm. Today the alarm was a heavy metal song titled, "The fireflies stole my light." He did his routine chores and as he was about to leave for office, he received a phone call. He answered the call.

He listened to the voice from the other end, "23rd, right? Yes, I remember. I will be there." He locked the house, put on his helmet, and vroomed his way out into the bright day. He did not observe a woman standing outside her house in the veranda, frantically searching for her husband who was nowhere to be found.

Today Kiran reached quite early to the office. He decided to wait for Ravi in the parking space. To spend the time, he started to browse through a few dance videos on YouTube. He watched a ballet performance and replaying a pirouetted swing of the dancer. Her legs were in the air and when she landed, she twirled again. That twirl brought memories. He continued to watch the video, but in his head, something else played.

He was seven years old. He was watching a *Kathak* performance on TV. Most of the boys of his age watched cartoons or *Shaktiman* on TV. But he watched dance performances on Doordarshan. He started to mimic the dancer. As the dancer whirled on the beat, he too whirled practising the leg movement and the hand movement of the dancer. He had almost perfected that move and was about to rush into the kitchen and tell his mother. The wide grin on his face turned into fear when he saw his father coming in.

His father was early today. He did not like dancing. He wanted his son to focus on studies. But instead, his son was crazy about dancing. As far as his father knew, boys do not dance. And the girls who danced were bad girls. Young Kiran stepped backwards trembling in fear. His father walked at a fast pace, held him by his shoulders and gave a tight slap. Kiran fell down yelping in pain. His mother came running from the kitchen. She tried to

shield her son from his father's wrath but today her husband was mad. He
yanked his belt and gave a crazy beating to Kiran. He also threatened him
that if he ever danced again, he would whip his back until he is dead.

Kiran's eyes were wet. He stopped the video and watched into the distance
before him. He could never forget that beating which his father gave him.
But that beating also made him stronger. Next time when his father had
caught him dancing, he removed his shirt and showed his back to the father.
He closed his eyes thinking that his father will beat the life out of him.
Instead, his father walked out of the room leaving the boy alone.

"Did you hear the latest news?" Ravi started his morning commentary
parking his bike in the lot.

Kiran sighed. Yesterday it was the dancer, today it is the murder. He started
walking with his friend not reacting to any of his friend's news updates. As
they stepped inside, Kiran resolved to get the pending vouchers signed and
approved by his Boss and file them away. And the MIS report that was
pending from last week must be done today.

Chapter - 4

Before four suitors and a thousand cups of coffee, Sravanya was hopeful of finding a worthy companion for herself. That was a long time back when she liked milk in her coffee. Now she liked it without milk and without sugar. She had started to like the tinge of bitterness in her life. How our tastes and preferences change! But the one thing that did not change an iota was her parent's love for her. And their strict daily routine which she termed as their daily regime. Nanna (Father) would get up early and go for a walk and while returning he would bring vegetables and fruits and other groceries. Amma (Mother) would clean the house first thing in the morning, take a bath, decorate the idols, and perform an hour-long morning Puja. Except those five days of the month when she would not enter the temple room, and the doors of the temple room remain would remain closed.

Sravanya was definitely not an atheist but she was not a hardcore deity worshipper either. Her faith was invested in social work. To her, serving the poor and needy was serving God. She was a double M.A. in *Kuchipudi* and in Anthropology. The two loves and passions of her life. In fact, she would joke to her mother, why do I have to marry? I have two husbands already, and I serve both of them well, my *pati parmeshwars*. But her mother was persistent - a physical husband is a must. And this was one of their daily talks, her mother coaxing her to get married. And the other thing was coffee. Her mother failed to understand why she liked it black. And so, she would also coax her daughter to have filter coffee with milk. As if the only two things that bothered her mother were her marriage and coffee with milk.

It was difficult to explain to her mother why she was not excited about marriage or did not like milk in her coffee. After a lot of persistent argument from her mother, she finally came up with three conditions - 1) The person she is intending to marry should be an artist. 2) He should be a bigger artist than her. 3) She should respect him wholeheartedly.

Her parents found a suitor who fulfilled all these three qualities, and yet it was a no from Sravanya. Having completed her morning dance routine, she settled on the big, wooden swing in their veranda. She wiped off the sweat from her forehead and her neck with the edge of her *sari*. Amma and Nanna settled in the cane chairs next to her, sipping their filtered coffee from a steel glass.

She took the mug on which was inscribed her favourite quote by Ayn Rand, "I swear by my life and my love of it that I will never live for the sake of another man, nor ask another man to live for mine." She took a long sip from her mug closing her eyes, relaxing her body and mind after a strenuous dance practice.

She could see her mother signalling her father. The marriage talks again. Today, the moderator of the discussion was Nanna, a welcome change from her mother's rigid dogmas. Nanna cleared his throat and spoke in a well-rehearsed tone, "Sraavi, doesn't Satya fulfill your three conditions? He is a bigger artist than you and you sure do admire him. In fact, he is one of your favourite music directors."

"He definitely makes good music. But most of the time he copies. I found about it very recently. And hence he has stepped down from my favourite music director's list," Sravanya put it plainly.

Nanna's eyebrow arched an inch higher and fell down clearly expressing his surprise and disappointment in Satya.

"Oh!" escaped from Nanna's mouth, and then he fell silent.

"I think to put it properly, it is called inspiration. And everyone needs some inspiration all the time," Amma tried her best to convince her daughter.

Sravanya, putting her mug back on the small cane teapoy, said, "He is not a bigger artist than me. And Amma, I agree everyone needs inspiration, but there is a difference between copying and inspiration, you know that. Just don't start a discussion for the heck of it."

"I mean, he earns well, he is respected all over. He has good manners and etiquettes, he likes you…" Amma could go on but she stopped at the angry glare from her daughter.

"He has to earn my respect first. Period." Sravanya shut her mother who picked up the empty mug and steel glasses and walked into the kitchen knowing it was pointless to speak anything now.

Nanna went back to reading the newspaper. Sravanya heard the rapid flipping of the newspaper pages and the sound of utensils from the kitchen.

Attraction is a rare phenomenon for Sravanya, like *Neela Kurinji* that blooms once in a decade. The flower of attraction bloomed first when she was twelve. It was for her Mathematics teacher, her first crush. Leaning a little backwards and adjusting her back on the pillow on the large wooden swing, the image of Arvind Meka, her Maths teacher, filled her mind.

He was not someone who stood out or had a great physique. He was like any other Maths teacher, strict and the very sight of him made his students shudder. Sravanya had failed in Maths in the unit test that academic year. Naturally, concerned over her daughter's grades, her father had asked Arvind to take home tuitions in the evening after school, and Arvind readily agreed as he could use the extra money. Sravanya became even more scared. Maths was difficult to comprehend and now the evening time would be filled with Maths and not dance.

At the beginning, it was as difficult following her teacher as it was in the school. But Arvind Meka did not give up. He would devise new and simpler ways of teaching his student. Knowing that Sravanya loved dancing, he would give examples from dance to make Maths interesting to her. Once he had explained to her how the rhythm on which the dance steps were based and the speed at which it changed, he had shown her to calculate the speed and the movement of her steps.

Not only that, he explained to her how Sanskrit language itself was based on Mathematics. He taught her Vedic Mathematics and different shortcuts to help her remember the formulas and apply them in the tests. She had started to enjoy his lectures and Maths too. Once a gibberish language to her, Maths had now started to make sense.

She regarded him as an artist. Not that people generally thought Maths as an art. But for her it was a difficult craft and her teacher mastered it and brought a lot of innovation to it. And when he was lost in explaining the principles of algebra or a simple Maths problem, his fingers danced to the rhythm of his voice. Arvind had this habit of using hand gestures a lot while talking. His fingers were long and beautiful. Sometimes, Sravanya would just lose herself watching his fingers dance. Seeing his student lost in some reverie, he would bang the wooden scale on her table to bring her back to reality. But never did he use it on her. It was always a scolding in which Sravanya saw only affection.

More than Arvind's face, she remembered those nimble fingers that created different shapes and forms and figures while he taught her. Till date, she had never seen any man with such beautifully sculpted fingers. Sometimes, she wondered, if she had a fetish for fingers? Arvind Meka had resigned from his job after teaching her for two years and no matter how hard she tried to trace him after she went to college, she could not find any trace of him. She tried looking him up in social media accounts but there too she could not find him.

Even if she found him what would she say after all these years? "Sir, I enjoyed your classes, not for the Maths, but your fingers, and the way they danced." She smiled at her thought. Were there any other men whom she had found so attractive? Her first crush was her Maths teacher, and her second crush which was a little more than a crush happened almost after a decade. And what was she doing in all those ten years between her two crushes not getting attracted to a man? Does that mean that she had to wait for another decade to just have that streak of attraction, leave alone falling in love?

Yazaan, the n is silent, he had said. And the way he had said his name itself felt like a song. Sravanya, double stress on n, she had blabbered. And for the next five minutes, they had spent teaching each other how to pronounce their names. It was a very wet evening.

The streets of New York were clogged with taxis and people trying to hail cabs to escape the rain. Sravanya loved the rain. But the streets were too crowded, and the traffic sounds annoyed her. She slipped into a diner for an early dinner enjoying the view through the windows of the diner situated in the most happening part of the city. The diner was crowded too, she got a seat after an hour's wait.

Yazaan sat opposite her and introduced himself. She knew him from the University, he attended the same class that she attended, "The Extinct Tribes of the world" on Thursdays. She was doing her Masters in Anthropology; he was doing his Masters in Music. That moist evening in New York was just the start of their friendship.

Yazaan was an African-American singer, wore thick glasses and sported an Afro hairstyle. His dream was to embed African folk music into mainstream music. He sang several songs from his tribe to Sravanya during their evening walks together. He talked about Africa, and Sravanya talked about India. He would attend her dance drama programs, and she would attend his performances in the local bars where he would sing African songs to jazz.

Slowly swinging herself swing in the veranda, she reminisced her time with him. Her father had disappeared into the kitchen probably to console her mother and give her hope. That one evening with Yazaan was the most beautiful memory and also the most painful. They were sitting on a bench next to the river watching the seagulls. The cold breeze had flushed her cheeks.

Yazaan sang a beautiful love song, she did not understand the meaning of it then, but later on he had explained to her what it meant. The song was a proposal from a man to a woman of his tribe for marriage. About how he would love her till the end of the time. His voice had filled the beautiful evening. She could not understand the words, but she understood the melody, the tune. She hummed the tune now as Yazaan's voice filled her.

What she also remembered was how emotional she felt that evening. She had felt love brushing her heart through that one song. She brimmed with ecstasy. She felt like the flowing river, she flew like the seagull, a calming peace ran through her veins. It was a feeling that she never felt after that. She was so much in love with Yazaan's spirit that she couldn't contain herself. She had become one with his song, with his voice. She became his song. There were tears in her eyes.

After the song was over, she had said, "I could feel your love, your soul. Your tears flow through my eyes."

Yazaan had smiled at her, and said, "I felt you too Sravanya." He always pronounced her name in African American lingo which irritated her, but today it didn't bother her. "I swore to my tribe leader that I would marry a woman from my tribe. I can't break it. But know this, you would be the only woman who touched my soul."

Even if Yazaan broke his promise, her parents would never agree. And she did not have it in her to oppose her parents. They never discussed love and marriage after that. They remained as friends, and after they had completed their masters, they both went different paths. They never wrote letters or emails. Their memories of each other had become a part of them.

Yazaan's voice never left her. She had taught Yazaan *Gayatri Mantra* and Ganesh *stotra* which Yazaan sang at an Inter-cultural arts conference receiving a standing ovation. She had recorded all of Yazaan's songs and listened to them whenever she felt lost.

That was a few years back, when she loved milk in coffee. And it was with Yazaan that she started liking black coffee as a kindred spirit. For many days she was hopeful that she would find a kindred spirit in India, if not in her own caste, in a different caste agreeable to her parents. But the upper caste guys she met were far away from coming a notch closer to a kindred spirit, they were all decadent souls trying to win a rank in the materialistic elements of life. And she was of the elements of nature.

She had realised it very soon after she was back from the States that she can't count upon for that one person to shake the earth beneath her feet and show her something different in life. She won't be feeling the way she felt like that evening in the near future and it was very likely going to be never.

Unable to convince her parents of maintaining a single status, she agreed to meet the suitors. They were charming fellows mesmerised with her beauty and unappreciative of her talent. One of them who was selected after a lot of screening and a few cups of coffee seemed promising enough. But it wasn't very late that he showed his true face. He had permitted Sravanya to continue dancing after marriage, but no stage shows or dancing in public. However, she could teach a few students if she was so inclined to dance.

"After marriage ladies anyway won't have much time left," he had said on their dinner meet. "You will be busy taking care of the kids." Sravanya was so angry that she felt like throwing the hot soup over his face.

She simply said, "So kind of you to give me permission to dance." The whole evening, she ate dinner without speaking a word.

The suitor kept asking her, "Did I say anything wrong?"

She shook her head and kept munching the food.

Back home her mother asked, "When he was asking you so many times, you should have at least told him what you felt."

Sravanya explained, "A man who does not understand that dancing should be my choice and not his, I felt talking sense into him was a futile exercise. I would rather enjoy the dinner than the company."

The second suitor was better, he did not have a problem with her dancing. But he was worried about her anthropology and social work. His concern was that if she were to remain engaged all the time in her dance performances and anthropology work, they would have little family time. And he was not ready to change his career plans for Sravanya. He was the one who brought a fat package home and hence his career and ambitions should be her first priority.

There were two other finalists in the groom-race and Sravanya did not like either. Vexed with her parents' relentless quest for the groom, she came up with three conditions. In the beginning her parents thought it was easy to find a groom who met all the three conditions but as time went by, they realised their daughter had put up the most complex clause. More than their daughter they themselves waited for the right person to come into their daughter's life.

Sravanya cared the least for the right person to come her way, she was worried more about the wrong things that were happening in her town.

Another murder in her town. She switched on the TV to get the recent updates. The medical officer in his autopsy report has declared that death was because of the heavy fall on the steps and multiple injuries on the head.

But what the hell that man was doing at midnight in the fort? Why did he even go there?

The journalist in the TV was showing a graphical representation of how the guy fell on the steps, hit his head and died. This was not a murder, but the police could not fathom why he would walk out of his house in the night and went up to the fort.

The damn fort was again in the news.

It was one of the tourist spots of the town and Sravanya knew how the village's *sarpanch* was trying to increase tourism and had applied for government grants. Was someone sabotaging his plans willfully? Another dead body at the fort was definitely not something that would encourage tourists. The government would put a ban on the release of the funds until this was sorted out. And who was the person who would benefit most from the bad publicity of their town?

She called out to her parents, "Amma- Nanna, I am going out to meet Mamayya (Uncle). Have something urgent to discuss."

Chapter - 5

Several newspapers were laid across on the teapoy in front of Parasuram.

He looked at them and then gazed towards the front yard. His deep set eyes had a grim and stern yet a distinct determined look. He was drowned in his thoughts as his thick brows furrowed. He gently rubbed his forehead and let out a soft sigh.

Bangaru Babu came out from the kitchen and stood near Parasuram. "Mamayya, may I bring coffee for you?" he asked. Parasuram looked at him and smiled softly before shaking his head.

Bangaru Babu was an orphan. His parents died when he was just fifteen years old and from then onwards, Parasuram had asked him to come and stay at his house during the daytime. Bangaru Babu was quite helpful as well as he helped Parasuram's wife, Malati in household work. He did all the household work such as cleaning and cooking and sometimes would even go out to bring some urgent grocery items. Parasuram cherished Bangaru Babu since he and Malati didn't have any kids. Malati's time was usually spent around praying and doing community service.

"No, a journalist is coming. Bring coffee after he comes," Parasuram said. Bangaru Babu nodded before he walked off to the kitchen.

*****

The journalist Subramanyam lived in a nearby village and was very fluent in Telugu. He worked for the Telugu newspaper, *Andhra Velugu,* and his reports and features appeared in the district supplement of the newspaper almost every day. His family was proud of him but Subramanyam knew that he still had a long way to go.

Subramanyam had called Parasuram the previous evening asking the latter if they could meet up sometime to discuss the situation about the recent killings. Parasuram replied that the journalist could just interview him on the phone but Subramanyam insisted that he wanted to grab this chance to meet him.

"*Mamayya,* I just want to use this opportunity to meet you. It's been so long..." Parasuram wasn't really Subramanyam's *Mamayya.* That's just what everyone in the town and neighbouring places -- from servant to the journalist -- called him with much affection. Years ago, he was the chief guest at a poetry session and given his nature, he praised a young poetess for her poems. The young poetess then addressed Parasuram as Mamayya and soon after, he was Mamayya for everyone in the community.

Parasuram was never an elected politician nor was he a government appointee for any post. His selfless dedication towards the welfare of the community and a reliable person for anybody who was in any sort of need or in trouble made him the unofficial leader of the town. He never said no to anyone. Over a period of time, he exerted a tremendous influence on the whole town becoming a moral and spiritual guru for everybody.

Parasuram was in fact a bit tired of the journalists' itch to write whatever that came to their minds. He had read only one of the newspaper articles in front of him. Its headline screamed: *The town head has no interest in its well-being and has no competence in finding the culprits*! Parasuram was so disgusted that he did not bother to read the articles in the remaining newspapers. The only consolation was that *Andhra Velugu* had a small factual report. That newspaper did not resort to sensationalism and it was one of the reasons why Parasuram agreed to meet Subramanyam.

*****

Subramanyam arrived on his scooter sharply at 9 am and walked inside through the open door. Bangaru Babu appeared and Subramanyam greeted him. Bangaru Babu took the journalist to where Parasuram was seated. Parasuram's aura was kingly and authentic and for a moment Subramanyam was in awe. Parasuram glanced back at the journalist and stood up. They both greeted each other with *namaste*s. Parasuram gestured to Subramanyam to sit on the chair opposite his.

"Mamayya, my newspaper has commissioned me to write a scathing report on the current situation and I'm just doing my job," Subramanyam said.

"*Manchidi* (Good), Subramanyam. Just do your job," Parasuram smiled softly. His smile helped Subramanyam's heart calm down a little as it was beating too fast before. Parasuram glanced back at the house and shouted, "Bangaram, get two cups of coffee!"

Subramanyam pulled out a pen and a notebook from his bag and began the recording on his phone as well.

"Mamayya, what do you think of the murders?" Subramanyam asked.

"Very ghastly, very devastating. I am not able to digest the events."

Subramanyam wrote down the keywords in his notebook. Bangaru Babu was quick enough to bring coffee and biscuits on a tray. He placed them on the teapoy and left. Parasuram gave one cup to Subramanyam and took the second one. Subramanyam began to sip his coffee while recording with his right hand.

"The police are investigating," Subramanyam said.

"Yes, I know."

"But there's no headway."

"Yes, I can understand. We are a small town," he said and paused. "Actually, a big village. We don't have a huge number of resources. The post-mortems, forensic reports all take time, they have to come from the district headquarters or the state capital."

"The people are spreading rumours that you are not doing your bit; you have neither the interest nor the competence to solve the problem."

Parasuram's expression changed ever so slightly. He tried not to show it though. "What do you want me to do? The police are doing the best to give them the credit. They are not neglecting the matter."

"Do you have any suspects in mind?"

"All people in our town are good people," Parasuram said.

Subramanyam frowned a little and clutched onto his pen and notebook tighter. "Do you mean someone from other places is coming here to murder our people? Which place?"

Parasuram sipped his coffee and kept his features as soft as possible. "The name of a place comes into question if the murderer is a human, right?" he asked, measuring his words carefully.

Subramanyam gasped. "I-is there a ghost in our village killing our people?!"

Parasuram gazed into the sky and sighed softly. "All I can say is, it does not look like the work of a human. Non-human could mean animal as well."

Subramanyam sat erect now. He gazed deeply into Parasuram's eyes and wished he could get as much information as he can today. "This is a headline statement. Can you please elaborate, Mamayya?"

"At the moment, I don't have anything more to add. As I know more, I will call you and let you know," Parasuram said. "Let's finish our coffee."

Subramanyam smiled. He knew that he wouldn't be able to extract anything more from Parasuram anymore because of his body language and his tone. A few minutes later, Subramanyam finished his coffee, gave his *namaste* and left.

*****

Parasuram's heart and shoulders felt heavy. The burden he was carrying was unusual and seemed totally unfair. His mind whirled with mismatched thoughts; sometimes he would think one thing and the other times, he would think about a completely off topic situation. He wasn't in his usual state of mind, for all that matters.

Parasuram had dreamt of developing this small town, Kotagiri. Until recent past it was a village and modern developments made it look like a town of sorts. The hills, the woods and the fort could, in fact, be developed as a tourist destination. Not that it was not a tourist destination currently. But the place was ruined, some part of it had to be restored, built up. There were a few tourists now and then, and the town's tourist income was very meagre. Even the devotees that visited the temple were not that many compared to other temples. He wanted to popularise the temple like the temples of Khajuraho, making it a cultural and art destination. He wanted to develop the wasteland behind the fort into a blooming garden, build a small pond, erect great statues. He also needed money to build roads and repair the steps of the fort to make it more accessible. All these required funds. People could enjoy their time with their family or friends, and they would always be welcome to come here to get away from the hustle and bustle of cities and breathe in some fresh air. But as of today, neither the fort, nor the temple had the infrastructure and the facilities.

He had been making the representations to the legislator and other politicians in the district. Just as his efforts seemed to bear fruit, these killings began to happen. Not in a million years did Parasuram think that something like this would take place. His place was meant to be the epitome of purity and tranquillity, but now that image was being mercilessly trampled.

Parasuram walked towards his study room, unbolted the doors and pushed them open. The doors had been closed for quite some time so they squeaked as they swung behind. He entered the room. It was a square room, eight by eight feet and looked like a mini library.

On the opposite side of the doors was a closed window and abutting it were a desk and a chair. Parasuram opened the window and let in some sunlight and fresh air. He looked at the empty street for a couple of minutes before going through the books, files and papers on his shelves and cabinets.

Parasuram knew that there was some material in the room that would reinforce his hunch. But what was it? He could not put his finger on it, but he was sure it was there. He just needed to look hard and look fast.

As he went through shelf after shelf and pile after pile of papers, the memories of government apathy towards the town's development and himself running from pillar to post ran at the back of his mind like an old record. As though someone had finally managed to dust the turntable and play Parasuram's favorite song.

However, as hours passed, Parasuram couldn't find any papers that he thought he would find. The birds were singing but he couldn't enjoy it one bit.

Should I give up...? he thought as he sat on the chair and sighed softly. *Maybe there is nothing in here to corroborate my suspicion.* He began wondering. *I am sixty-two now but when I was younger, I had such a vivid memory and could remember exactly where every item of my paraphernalia was kept.*

Parasuram inhaled deeply and motivated himself a little. *If my mind has thought of some kind of background material then surely it is there in this very room. I just have to trust my mind more than anything else in the world.*

Parasuram stood up and doggedly continued his search for any kinds of hints or clues. Sweat dripped from his forehead and temples. His breathing was shallow and even though the windows were open, he felt as though he was stuck inside a closed box.

Parasuram was forced to take several breaks near the window to catch his breath. He just wanted to sit down. Or better yet, lie down and take a nap but he wouldn't do so. Not until he found what he was looking for. He wasn't the type to give up so easily.

*****

Human memory is indeed so fickle; one minute it's mute, completely in the dark and then the next, it sings like a parrot. It's like our memory plays hide and seek with us. It teases us, pulls our leg and even betrays us sometimes like all our exes.

To Parasuram, it came like a flash that couldn't have been possible if he didn't spend hours searching the room like a mad man. He wasn't going to let his memories play a prank on him any longer.

A few months ago, Parasuram had told Bangaru Babu to keep some vessels and boxes up in the attic. Those were just pieces that were lying around in the house. Some were Malati's which she didn't use or had bought and forgot to use and some were Parasuram's. He wasn't a hoarder, but he couldn't part with the little things either because they were of sentimental value. He had also told Bangaru Babu to fill in one of the cardboard boxes that was half full.

At once, Parasuram rushed out of the room, brought in a ladder and climbed the attic. He saw four cardboard boxes and brought them down one by one. His bones and muscles ached but the more his memory flashed before his eyes, the quicker he wanted to rip open the boxes. Bangaru Babu had kept the boxes in the attic but hadn't labeled any of them.

Parasuram squatted on the floor and caught his breath. The brown tapes were already coming off so Parasuram had to just rip them off and open the flaps.

The first two boxes were filled with nothing but books and a couple of stationery items but in the third box, Parasuram found three significant things. One, an old diary by a British officer with a few loose pages of the diary notes that were translated into Telugu; he recalled getting the translations done when he was in his twenties. Second, there was a very old newspaper article of a fortune teller foreboding bad omen for the town in 2021, which at first Parasuram didn't believe but had kept because his gut had told him that it was going to be useful. Lastly, his own handwritten notes and a photo of stones with inscriptions and sculptures on it.

Parasuram drew his reading glasses from the top of the desk. He carefully read and reread the documentation and slowly but surely everything fell into place.

He was able to reconstruct the past; a past which told him a story; a story of bigotry and hatred, of indifference and cruelty; a cruelty that now came to haunt his beloved town, a town he loved so dearly was now set to become the victim of brutal and macabre acts.

*****

Sravanya's voice pierced through the veil of time bringing Parasuram back to the current time. He was still holding onto the yellow torn pages of the diary when Sravanya came into his room, "Mamayya, are you cleaning your room?"

The images that had formed from reading the diary diminished and disappeared into the sunlight, but his mind was hazy. Putting the diary back into the cardboard box, "We must find a solution else it would be too late," was all he could manage to say.

Sravanya, clueless of what Parasuram was talking, interpreted it in her own way. "I think the head priest Sadanand Sastri is behind this and we must warn the police to look into him."

"That's a big accusation?" Parasuram frowned and waited for Sravanya to explain.

Sravanya sat next to him on the floor theorizing what could be Sastri's motive, "We should think from the angle of who tends to gain the most if the town is blacklisted as a tourist place. I remembered today morning that when we submitted to the Tourism office a plan for the restoration of the fort and other places but not the temple, Sastri voted against us and wanted that all the funds should go to the temple alone."

"So? He cooked up a crooked plan about murdering people." Clicking his tongue, he showed his disapproval. "And when did you become a detective from a dancer?"

"I might be wrong but what's the harm in looking into every possible alternative. You know that there is a second murder."

"It was not a murder. It was an accident."

"I know. The second victim died falling from the steps of the fort. But Mamayya, what was he doing there at that hour of the night? Isn't it fishy?"

Parasuram rubbed his hair and looked into the sunlight trying to clear his head. Of course, there was something fishy. But not what Sravanya thought. It was not the play of mortal man. But he fell short of words to explain his theory to her. It was good having Sravanya here. Her presence itself uplifted his spirits.
While all the women of her age were busy finding the suitable groom to get married or were busy fulfilling their duties as wives and mothers, Sravanya catered herself to community work and welfare of the *Mandal*. He smiled at her affectionately.

"We must go now to the police station and update ourselves regarding the latest status. And also give an indirect tip to the police about who all might be against the building of the town into a bigger tourist destination including Sastri Sir."

Without waiting for an answer from Parasuram, she called Bangaru Babu who appeared in the room within seconds. "We are going to the police station." Bangaru Babu nodded.

As they were about to leave, Bangaru Babu said, "*Akka*, did you see the newspaper today. Already, one journalist has remarked that Mamayya is not interested in solving the murders."

Sravanya looked back, "I know. Nanna told me while I was leaving for here. Don't worry. They will change their words."

*****

At the police station, the SI, Suresh Pidugu, who was in charge of the case was an oversized man, his tummy the size of a pot, the button of his shirts overburdened by his size and felt like they would explode any time. Suresh

Pidugu was more interested in the betel nut pan he was chewing than the case.

When Sravanya told him that they should also look into different alternatives including the funding from the State Tourism Board and a detailed search of the fort, he nodded in banal affirmation which was not encouraging at all. Spitting thickly into the dustbin at his feet he remarked, "The second one is not a murder at all and hence this does not make a serial case. The first murder was of a tourist. It is possible that one of his friends might have murdered him. We are investigating the group thoroughly. I think both of you should not worry so much giving it a new controversy angle. Already, the journalists have come up with many more creative theories than you Madam." He looked sharply at Sravanya.

She was about to blast him but Parasuram intervened, "Inspector, we expect that your team will do the best in finding the killer. Do not hesitate to reach out to me or Sravanya in case you need any help or need information." With that, he stood up with a *namaste* and walked out. Sravanya also followed him. The inspector spit again into the dustbin.

"What a waste of a trip?" she muttered as they got into her car. She drove slowly out of there still thinking about the inspector. She was not at all convinced that they would catch the killer soon. What should she do next? They can't wait for another murder. And how stupid it sounded when the inspector was defining a serial murder case.

"Sravanya, the police cannot catch the murderer," Parasuram said, cutting the thread of her thoughts.

She didn't say anything.

"Because the murderer is not a mortal being," Parasuram said picking his words carefully.

"What?"

"I will tell you a story from an old diary I found this morning."

Chapter - 6

With the grace of a swan, they danced. Long arms extended to the ceiling, fingers reaching out as though touching a veil. The music was not there, yet was there, with a soft ease that enveloped the dancer. They're one. The music and the movements born together in a moment of frivolity and fancy.

Images were reflected at the mirrors that line the front of the room which guided the dancer through the steps. No faults went unfixed, no moment went unnoticed. Theirs were the only eyes on the performance. All judgement, all praise, all perspective came from a single set of eyes, but the precision to which they hold themselves kept them on track.

The song in the mind crescendoed, the movements grew frantic. A twist, a leap, a landing that fell into a pirouette so polished that one would liken it to a pebble smoothed by many years in the ocean. With a final flourish, the dance came to a rounding end, and the dancer slowed to a stop.

The energy that once energised Bhushan drained, replacing the quiet serenity with exhaustion. Looking up, they allowed their eyes to trace over their features. The dark patches of stubble that tries to claim them a man, the toned muscles that line the body not hidden beneath the clothes chosen to dance with. The shoulder-length black hair that fell from the strip of fabric used to hide it away so that it did not distract as they danced.

The world thinks of me as a man. And by all appearances, that's what I am.

Bhushan blinked and turned their head to avoid the burn. The early morning sun brought a glaring brightness into the mirrors of the room. This, for Bhushan, was usually the time to leave. When the sun came up, the village awakened.

With their skin slicked with sweat, the early morning chill that hangs in the air was a refreshing welcome. With the sun making its way up in the sky, the warm glow allowed Bhushan to see their reflection in the mirror.

With hands held like they were holding a book open, they pushed against their chest and cup the unrelenting flesh there. Being a dancer, Bhushan had little in the way of fat, but their hands gathered what they could and pushed up. The petite breasts thus created offered warmth of contentedness. It's proof that inside, the person they know they are, is waiting to be found and presented to the world. The nipples stiffened a bit and they imagined prolonged ones.

This is who I want to be.

Satisfied with what they could see, Bhushan squatted down to pee.

I am a woman.

After washing their hands, Bhushan stretched one last time before returning home.

*****

Despite the early hour, their parents were outside in the fields. There are countless animals that needed to be fed, crops that must be tended to, and a long list of repairs that need to be made to the barn and the equipment stored inside.

A farmer's work is never done, Bhushan's father would proclaim regularly. *Then why have we become farmers*, Bhushan would internally reply. Their thoughts and feelings on the matter, however, didn't play into it. They are farmers, so Bhushan must respect that. They must play their part. And so, with the last remaining vestiges of contentedness, they finished their hastily made breakfast and headed out into the fields to assist their mother in feeding the animals.

Lunch time rolled around just as the sun reached its peak. They ate alone. Dirt caked the skin on Bhushan's fingers, and an ache radiated around their feet. Nothing unusual. Every day is the same, but the mundanity of Bhushan's life was not something they complained about. The familiarity of their routine also offered safety.

"There will be a sacrifice today." Bhushan looked up from washing their hands and looked over at their uncle who had just come in.

"Mamayya, what do you mean?"

"Today, at the temple, before the sun goes down, a girl will be offered before the God."

Such things were not unheard of in their village. In fact, Bhushan was wholly familiar with the idea, having heard about them in the past. A month ago, a *devadasi* passed away from old age. They knew this was coming. The whole village did.

What bothered Bhushan today was that they wanted to be the one who was dedicated to the God. *I deserve it.*

Bhushan helped the family with a few more menial chores around the farm and home and before long they all washed up and were ready for their journey to the temple. For most, the journey was arduous. The temple was atop a mountain so it caught the sun no matter the time of day. The steps were many and the sweat that has been spilled upon the hard stone could fill a lake.

Fortunately, for a family of farmers whose business it was to work all day in physical labour, Bhushan, Mamayya, Mother and Father approached the stairs with none of the trepidation that the others in the village may face. Though it takes near enough an hour to reach the peak, they were neither out of breath nor sweating as much as the others.

"Today we offer up a virgin to the God in the hopes that we will be blessed for another year." The girl, the *devadasi* now, was a slender slip of a thing, dressed in a bright coloured fabrics and a gentle face. She stepped into the centre of the temple with not an ounce of nerves or anxiety evident in her demeanour. The *devadasi* swore her life to the temple and to serve there until her dying days. To be gifted to the deity, God or temple was a high honour. One that Bhushan wanted so badly they could taste it.

I could be her.

"Such grace in this young woman." Father was heard whispering.

The music continued and gripped Bhushan. It threw them into a rhythm, like the wind catches a leaf, and for an unforgiving moment, they could not control themselves. They needed to dance. They need to follow the music. They *must* become a *devadasi*.

"You were quiet today, my boy," Mamayya said as they stepped back inside.

Mother and Father retired to bed the moment they returned home, the hard day in the field mixed with the unexpected trip to the temple exhausted them beyond the norm. Bhushan, however, had too many things on their mind to consider sleep.

"Today was a long day Mamayya."

"Indeed."

The coming days were long, and much the same as the last. Bhushan would dance until the sun rose, work until lunch time and then work again until the time for sleep came. It was a familiar routine, and not one they hated.

When something came along to upset the day-to-day adventures, however, it was welcomed with enthusiasm. "A marriage procession will move through the village today, Bhushan, attend with me?" Mamayya gestured at the door and after receiving a nod of approval from their parents, Bhushan joined their uncle in the short walk to the village road.

"We will watch from the veranda," Father called. "A lovely day for such an event," Mother remarked. "Yes," Mamayya agreed.

The music fed through the people and trees, greeting the family with a soft flow that threaded into Bhushan's veins. This time, there was no controlling it. They're pulled, swayed and enraptured by the sound until they feel possessed. Slowly, they gave up attempting any restrain and simply flowed with the music. The expressions were small. A hand twisting in with the rhythm, a knee jutting out to the side so that they may lean on it and twist out their other foot.

From behind, where they cannot see, Mother watched on with surprised appreciation. She had always known her son enjoyed dancing, but she never saw. She and her husband never had the time, nor the money to spare, so indulging in their only child's whimsical hobbies seemed foolish.

Now, however, she wondered whether it was foolish to have not attended to his talents and helped them flourish. With a sharp elbow, she nudged her husband and threw a hand in the direction of their son. Together, they watched and nodded.

"You have a talent son," Father said.

"Dancing is a great expression of our bond with the gods," Bhushan announced.

The answer was the correct one, they observed in the smiles their parents offered in return. The burn in their cheeks was certainly a proud one, and Bhushan knew that pride can quickly become a sin.

Once the procession was gone, Bhushan said, "I would like to visit Mamayya's house."

"If he allows it," Mother said in a lighter vein.

"Always, for my favourite nephew."

The air was humid. Enough that Bhushan's breath seemed cold and wet. Haggard, even. Like their lungs had a hard time taking in any air. Or maybe it's not the air at all. Maybe it was the sudden realisation that today they want to talk to Mamayya about how they feel. How, while on the outside they may appear to be a man, on the inside they are not.

"Mamayya, I have something serious I would like to discuss with you."

"You are most welcome to share with me any thoughts you may have, nephew. I have made it my job to be your confidant."

Words were thick on their tongue. It was hard to swallow past the nerves that prickled against their skin. "I do not believe I am a man."

Surprisingly, Mamayya simply laughed riotously in response. "Oh, young Bhushan, your time will come for your manhood to be accepted. Sometimes it is before, sometimes it is after, but it will come."

"No, Mamayya. Not for me. It is not that I feel I have not grown into a man, yet. It is that I am not a man. Inside, in my heart, I know I am a woman. I cannot continue with this pretence for much longer. I feel I must be honest with someone, anyone, about my heart's feelings. I do not care to hold this illusion for much longer. I will leave and live out my true self somewhere where I will be accepted."

Mamayya froze in his chair, watching as his nephew pushed away from the table. It was only when Bhushan stood, turning towards the door, those words returned to him and were joined by sense a moment later.

"Bhushan, where are you going? You cannot leave like this! We must discuss these feelings. You're confused, surely you understand that?"

"I am not confused. I am very sure of myself. I know you won't accept me; I know my parents will not accept me either. I am not confused, but you all are woefully under-prepared for what I am."

Mamayya had heard enough, something that became obvious in the way he grabbed Bhushan's arm to prevent them from leaving. "You cannot simply leave. Where do you intend to go?"

"To the temple. I will live out my days as a *devadasi* with the others. The ordinary person may not be able to recognise who I am, but I know that the gods will."

Bhushan was confident in their decision. The world seemed to be a little less constricting as they stepped out onto the cobbled streets of their humble village. No longer were they a part of this menial way of life. No longer will they linger on the way of thinking that is beneath their religion. No longer will they endure this angst. The gods will see them for what they are, a woman in the body of a man against their will.

"Please don't go. Let us talk about this. Give me time, I will help. Things done in haste are done without care."

Mamayya's heavy footsteps followed him across the street.

"I have made my decision," Bhushan retorted effortlessly.

The temple was as beautiful and as imposing as it was the week before when they attended the *devadasi* ceremony. The stone walls as they stepped into the lobby were imbued with ancient energy that vibrated through the air and left Bhushan humming. This is the place where my heart is seen before my face, Bhushan decided.

"Son?" Bhushan turned on the ball of his foot, twisting around to face the priest.

"Priest, I have come to talk with you."

"You have? Well then, by all means, follow me. I shall have tea made and we may converse together."

Warmth swelled up inside Bhushan's chest at the presentation of a perfect opportunity to explain who they were and what they wanted. The priest will understand, because he is a harbinger of the gods' word. The gods know what is right and what is wrong. They will understand who Bhushan is and what they can represent to the temple.

Bhushan followed the priest through dark hallways. The candles have not yet been lit, as the sun is not down all the way. The clouds overhead, however, darkened the sky. It was dark enough to send a thrill of fear through Bhushan.

"Into my room please." Bhushan settled upon a deep red cushion, crossing their legs. The priest mirrored the actions and methodically prepared tea. Bhushan watched in patience, knowing that it's not uncommon for such a process to be sacred to a priest, or really any person in their part of the world.

"What brought you to this temple? What do you need to discuss?"

"I want to become a *devadasi*."

The silence that exploded following the statement was charged with confused caution. Bhushan watched, hoping to see understanding or acceptance, but the longer the priest went without speaking, the longer Bhushan became certain they wouldn't hear anything that they want or need to hear.

"Boy, you understand that the honour of becoming a *devadasi* is one bestowed upon women only."

It's not a question, Bhushan noticed. It's a statement. Of course, Bhushan understood. It's not something that could conceivably escape their attention. Everyone knew that it was a job for a woman, but Bhushan *was* a woman.

"Priest, understand that only on the outside I am a man."

"Boy," the priest repeated, forcefully this time, "I have no time for your games."

"I'm not playing games, I'm …"

"Then you are confused!" the priest shouted.

He stood, knocking the table over and spilling hot tea onto the grey floor. With heaving breaths, the priest grabbed Bhushan by the ear, pulled them up from the ground and dragged them from the room.

"You are not to come here with your… your attempts to defy the gods. You have a demon inside you. I won't allow a demon inside my home."

Bhushan's ear ached with the strain, but the panic of the moment overrode any discomfort they may feel on a physical level. Inside, where their heart hammered relentlessly against their ribcage, a different kind of pain bloomed.

"Now leave here and if you attempt to return, I will see that you're incapable of doing so again."

Body slamming against the ground where the stairs stopped, Bhushan gasped. Their entire left side ached from the impact, their ear burnt from the priest's handling, but so did their eyes, with tears of disappointment.

Maybe the priest is not as close to the gods as he should be.

The walk back to the farm was a long one.

Each step was a reminder that Bhushan was banished from the place they had hoped to one day call home. Every meter was a step closer to where their parents expected them to work, get married, have children and then eventually die.

That was not a life they wanted for themselves. It's unfair that everything was laid out before Bhushan even had a say in anything. That rules were made for the world to follow, whether their heart sang a different song or not. Who decided these things? Which person deemed the world to be so evenly split between what a person looked like and who a person was?

Fury gripped at Bhushan's stomach as they stepped in through the front door.

The priest may not want Bhushan, but Bhushan was not going to take no for an answer.

*****

Morning rose with a list of chores. Today, Bhushan slept through their usual dance and woke only when their mother rapped her fingers on the door frame.

"Bhushan, time has come for you to wake up. Come along. I will make you some breakfast."

Food held no appeal. Even the idea of eating came with the onslaught of nausea. But Mother was a stickler for eating meals at the appropriate time of day. 'You're a growing man,' she would say, not knowing that Bhushan wanted nothing more to do with the body they were forced into at conception.

"After breakfast, you need to go to the *kirana* store. Got some errands to run."

Breakfast was short. Bhushan had no appetite, so they could not eat a lot. Despite Mother's warning glance and worried clicking of her tongue, she said nothing and simply saw Bhushan out of the door.

At the store, after making purchases, they turned back. Mamayya was coming towards the store. Bhushan greeted him.

"I understand you are frustrated, Bhushan, but so am I. What you speak of is unheard of, but I have spent the night considering your situation and devising ways which we may employ to circumnavigate your desires."

This was not what Bhushan was expecting.

"You spoke with the priest?" Mamayya spoke without showing any emotion.

"I did."

"What happened?"

Bhushan did not want to relive the event from the evening before, but if Mamayya planned to help, it's best to be honest with him. Maybe he can truly offer the help that Bhushan desperately needed.

"I visited the priest, explained my wishes, and I was kicked out. He accused me of having a demon inside me or wishing to defile the name of the gods. He did not understand, nor did he attempt to listen to me. I do not believe he speaks for the gods."

"The priest, much like everyone else, knows that it is not proper to want to become a woman."

A flame of fury ignited in Bhushan's stomach, as it always did when they were forced to defend themselves for simply being who they were. "I am like this, not out of choice but out of heart. I know the difficulties that arise in the disturbed dust of the revelation, but I cannot choose; this was chosen for me."

Mamayya's face twisted and Bhushan waited for the blow that he was certain would come. "Perhaps you can become a dancer, play the female roles in the dramas. You can do what you like to do and play the parts you wish to play, without all the problems that will appear if you were to tell people about your… it…, it's confusing."

"I'm not interested in simply playing a part, Mamayya. I'm not confused. It's everyone else that is confused."

Mamayya's mouth fell, eyes searched the room around him and then landed again on Bhushan with dropped shoulders.

"I want to be a woman. I want to be a *devadasi*. I know what people will think, I understand how people may not understand, but it does not matter how they react to my change. The only one this will affect is me."

"This is stretching things too far," Mamayya hissed. He dragged Bhushan by the arm into the corner of the store, away from perking ears.

"Dance is my calling," Bhushan insisted. Their back straightened, eyes narrowed and mouth set in a thin line. "I'm willing to fight until the end for this. It is my passion, my will, my right. I want to be wedded to God and to serve him at the temple. I wish to do social and spiritual service through dance."

"Lower your voice," Mamayya demanded.

"Why?"

"Because, child," Mamayya almost sneered, "there are many things you do not understand. Things you are too naive to have known. But allow me to illuminate you, before you make the biggest mistake of your life and drag your parents name through the mud."

His bruising grip on Bhushan's arm tightened and the two of them moved to an empty alleyway. Despite the distant bustle from the street, Mamayya kept his voice low and searched around them every few minutes, in case someone had taken it upon themselves to eavesdrop on their conversation.

"The temple dancers are not what you believe. They are not what anyone believes. The temple is compromised and those dancers are sent to engage in non-marital relationships with the rich and powerful. Anyone with money and the desire simply sends word to the temple and in exchange a dancer is sent to their doorstep. The 'price' is sent as a donation, and the village economy depends on it."

Shock in the form of ice tore through their veins, and their vision swam alarmingly fast. With a hand braced against the wall and with several heads of Mamayya floating before them, Bhushan attempted to settle their breathing.

"I understand that this is a shock Bhushan, but it is the truth. These relationships transcend beyond being 'company.' They are of a sexual nature."

"In the name of the gods, in the house of the deities, they participate in such vile, filthy acts?"

Righteous fury flew through Bhushan, threatening to burst out.

"You are too young, too inexperienced. The world beyond the confines of your home is darker than you believe. Please hear what I am saying. Allow it to curtail your desire of becoming a woman and a *devadasi*. It simply cannot work. You must recognise that, at the very least."

Mamayya's pleading barely registered with Bhushan, who was slowly picking apart everything they thought they knew about the world they lived in.

Maybe the old devadasi was corrupt, but I will not be. I can be different. I will live closer to the gods, serve them as is meant to be. "This is my fight, Mamayya. I will finish it."

Bhushan went to the temple again to talk sense into the priest. They were greeted with anger, which was expected. Bhushan didn't let it discourage them, though.

"You will make me a *devadasi*. You will let me live with the temple dancers. You may not know it, but the gods recognise me as being female. You should too."

"Did you not hear what I said before?" the priest spat.

"I don't care. You have to make me a *devadasi*. It is my right."

"You have no rights," the priest shrieked.

The volume of his voice knocked Bhushan back, but they stood tall once again.

"You are evil. You have fallen to temptation, and I will not allow the weak-willed to serve in these divine walls. Get out, before I throw you down the mountain for your trespasses. You cannot become a *devadasi*!"

The air grew charged with anger from both; Bhushan sucked in a lungful of air and screamed. "You do not know what I can do."

*****

Cool water rushed over Bhushan's feet. The pebbles that sat beside them on the bank of the canal were smooth in their shaking hands, and they twisted them flat in their hand and launched one after the other across the water. Some skipped, some fell beneath the surface.

The water did nothing to soothe the burning anger, nor did the rock skipping ease their mind from the horror of the dismissal. Things might not look very good right now, but it's got to improve. Without improvement, where will they be?

No, Bhushan thought. *Mamayya is wrong. There is a place for me. The gods know this, and so must I trust in them.*

The walk home passed by in a flash, but Bhushan wished they had taken their time. When they stepped into the house, a hush fell over, but not before a particular voice made Bhushan's stomach drop.

"You kick me from your home and believe you are welcome in mine?" Bhushan accused the priest.

"Bhushan! We do not speak to guests like that in our home," Father admonished.

"And he did not come into our house to speak ill of me?" Bhushan challenged, making direct eye-contact with the priest. "I do not wish for you to be here. You have no business with my parents."

"Sit down," Father ordered.

The chair creaked from the force of Bhushan throwing themselves into it. Their arms folded so tightly over their chest that it was hard to breathe. Or maybe that was just the panic that had bloomed so large it took up a substantial amount of space in their chest.

"Bhushan, why did you not speak with us about how you have been feeling?"

The panic exploded, becoming a solid weight that rested in Bhushan's lungs. This was not a conversation they were ready to have with their parents.

"Because he was speaking to me about it." All the heads in the room twist around to watch Mamayya's arrival.

"I came by to make sure Bhushan had not done anything rash after a heated conversation that we engaged in earlier this morning. I can see, by the presence of the priest, that my fears have been realised."

Mamayya lowered his head in respect of the priest and turned to Bhushan's parents, repeating the process.

"I would have told you, *bava garu* (brother-in-law), but I had hoped to deter him from his foolish and misguided attempts to worship at the temple in the place of a woman. He proved to be stubborn on the topic however. Which, I assume, is why the priest is with us today?"

"The boy came to see me again today, promising that he would get his way one way or another. I felt it was a threat to our temple, and on the way of life this village is accustomed to. What would they think if we were to disregard the rules of nature? His hopes are absurd and damaging."

Hot, prickly anger assaulted Bhushan. Heat flooded their face and as their eyes danced between each person, they discovered that none of them were paying Bhushan any attention. They're talking over Bhushan's head, as though they were not in the room.

"Before we involve the *panchayat*, let's find a way that we can convince him not to go down this route. The gods are on our side with whatever is right, so if we pray, we can help him to overcome these… these… desires." Mamayya didn't look at Bhushan, but Bhushan can tell that it is purposeful. "Our special prayers will call upon the gods for their help, will it not?"

With a cough, the priest drew the attention back to him. He nodded to Mamayya, offered a silent thanks to Bhushan's parents and then left without acknowledging Bhushan again.

The priest went to meet the village *poligar*, a rich *zamindar*. He is a man who controlled the goings on inside the village and had a militia to support the rulers in war. It was the responsibility of the *poligars* to supply militia to the ruler's army in times of war. The priest told him about Bhushan's desire, and he was worried due to Bhushan's threat. The *zamindar* assured him not to despair and he would take care of the matter.

Meanwhile, Bhushan raced to the temple. Without the priest to interfere, Bhushan can appeal to the gods regarding the guidance they need to achieve their life's dream.

The dance one must perform to connect with the gods was a complicated series of movements that was said to bring a person closer to the gods when performed on ancient grounds. This was Bhushan's goal. To create a bridge between themselves in the mortal world and the gods so that they may hear their plea and assist.

Bhushan closed their eyes, filling the chant of Om in their body, mind and soul. That evening, they were dressed in a red *sari* draped in the pyjama style, the way dancers dress up for practice. Their feet and hands were bordered by alta. Their lips were painted red, their eyes lined with dark *kohl*, and a red *bindi* adored their face. They were in their true form, and they were ready to perform the dance of their life which they had been practising for years. The chanting of the Om had filled their soul with the divine energy and gave the strength to perform the dance today. After they did the *Namaskaram*, they invoked Lord Nataraja in themselves. They started their dance with the Shiva *Ashtotharam*[17].

They chanted the different names of Shiva as their hands and legs performed the different *mudras* and *mandalams* portraying Lord Shiva in his different names.

Om Shulapanine Namah (He who holds the trident)!
Their body had become the Trishul.

Om Gangadharaya Namah (He who carries river Ganga)!
Their movements showed Ganga flowing from the tresses of Lord Shiva.

---

[17] An ode, eulogy for Lord Shiva praising him in 108 different names.

Om Haraye Namah (He who is the destroyer)
They had become the destroyer, their eyes wide, their tongue out.

Om Pameshwaraya Namah (He who is the divine lord)
They had become a tranquill mannequin.

After the Shiva *Ashtothram*, Bhushan offered a *Panchanga Namaskaram*[18] to the deity of the temple, standing up gracefully with renewed vigour. They tied the *ghungroo* to their feet and were ready for the next act. Now that they prayed to Lord Shiva, it was time for the Roudra *Tandavam*[19]. The temple hall was surrounded by pillars with the 108 *Karanas*[20] of Lord Shiva. Drawing inspiration from each of the Karna, they prayed to Lord Shiva to give them enough strength to perform the *Tandava* dance. This was their tribute to Lord Shiva, to please the God and allow them to serve the divinity through dance as *devadasi*. They could have chosen a lighter act, more graceful one, but they were angry. They wanted to transform all their rage into the dance act they were able to perform now. They wanted to become one with the ultimate Master of the Universe performing the cosmic dance. Eyes closed, phantom music filling their mind, Bhushan didn't notice the sound of the distant galloping of the horses approaching the temple. They were in a trance. They were drowned in Bhakti. They opened their eyes, red with rage, their face glowed in a frightening radiance. They looked like the Goddess Shakti herself obsessed with a temper like fire that only the gods could douse. They were both woman and man in the same form. They considered themselves as Ardhanareeswara. A wave of joy filled their heart cherishing how beautiful they were. They were the Prakrithi-Purush in true sense and they realised it fully that moment.

Jatatavigalajjala pravahapavitasthale
Galeavalambya lambitam bhujangatungamalikam
With his neck consecrated by the flow of water that flows from his hair,
And on his neck a snake, which is hung like a garland,

---

[18] Done mostly by women when she kneels down with palms joined together or touching the feet of the revered one in the front.
[19] Tandavam is the divine dance by the Gods. Performed in violent mood the dance is called Roudra Tandavam
[20] Karanas are the 108 key transitions in the classical Indian dance described in Natya Shastra.

One hand in *Mayura Hasta*[21] and the other in *alapadma*[22], Bhushan moved to the right on swift jumps on their toes, with a little high jump, and landing on this right leg positioned a little back and then swiftly changing to an *aramandi*[23], his hand in *Sarpa-Sisha*[24] moved like a snake's hood forming a graceful wave from their waist up to the face and slowly the two hands turning into a garland.

The soldiers alighted from the horses outside the temple and rushed with their swords. Bhushan twirled and swirled, his hands, legs, hips, neck, face, eyes all aligned in a dance wave, a cosmic energy passed through him, they took half rounds on their knees, their little-below- the-shoulder-length hair blowing in the wind like a fan around their body, sweat dripping from their forehead smearing the *bindi*, tears flowing from their eyes smudging the *kohl*, the alta on their palms scattered from the sweat, Bhushan looked from afar like a huge flame dressed in a red *sari* dancing in the temple.

The feet of the soldiers marching in heavy boots...
The alta decorated feet of Bhushan swinging and swaying in the air..
The swords unsheathed in the soldier's hands...
The hands personifying the *Trishula* and the third eye of the Nataraja.

tatvata chatvarajvaladhanajnjayasphulingabha
nipitapajnchasayakam namannilimpanayakam...
May we obtain the riches of the Siddhis from the tangled strands Shiva's hair,
Who devoured the God of Love with the sparks of the fire that burns on his forehead,

The temple door forced open by the soldiers...
The swift and deft movements of the skilled dancer...
The raucous sound of the soldiers organizing themselves in a killing mode...
The rhythmic beat of the *ghungroo*...

---

[21] One of the 28 single hand gestures in Bharatanatyam/Kuchupudi dance.
[22] One of the 28 single hand gestures.
[23] The demipile position in Bharatnatyam.
[24] One of the 28 single hand gestures in Bharatanatyam/Kuchupudi dance.

Eyes closed, phantom music filling their mind, Bhushan didn't notice the soldiers until they're dragged onto the flank of a horse.

*****

"No!" Bhushan screamed, thrashing.

A thick rope was wrapped tightly around Bhushan's chest, pinning their arms to their chest.

"Who are you? What do you want?"

"We are the village army, here on orders of the *poligar*. He's heard of your treacherous ways and we have been ordered to teach you a lesson."

The guards were notorious for their rough handling, and the *zamindar* was not known for his forgiving nature. If anything was perceived as a threat against the village, that threat was terminated.

"Please, whatever they are asking you to do, it is against the wish of the gods. If you harm a faithful servant, they will smite you. You will suffer."

The words were ignored. The horses galloped down the stairs with flawless grace, but Bhushan didn't have the ability to appreciate that. The only thought that entered their mind was that they may not see the end of the day.

"Please. Please, let me go."

The horses skidded into a stop, dust and rocks flying up behind them. The fort spread about before them. A large hand grabbed the ropes and yanked Bhushan down from the horse.

Without the use of their hands to balance themselves, Bhushan landed on the ground, their shoulder smacking into the rocks. A scream ripped from their throat, but a kick in the mouth quickly left Bhushan silently gasping as their shattered teeth pattered into the pool of blood that was rapidly growing around their face.

One of the guards, the strongest, knelt beside Bhushan. His hand roughly grabbed Bhushan's jaw, and fresh agony erupted as he squeezed.

"The *zamindar* ordered us to take care of you before your sins poison the crops of the village and damage our connection to the gods."

Without words to express how stupid those beliefs were, Bhushan was subjected to torturous beating. Thoughts of their parents, uncle, priest and friends flashed through their mind. *And what of dancing? Without their life, will their soul strengthened by dance live on? Is that possible?*

"Say goodbye to this world," someone said.

With terror, Bhushan's eyes flashed to a rock the size of a wheel coming down towards their face.

Chapter - 7

Around 5.45 pm on the 23rd, Ravi drove towards the government primary school and parked his bike outside the school gate. He pulled off his helmet and locked it on the bike handles.

The school atmosphere triggered a lot of memories of childhood; how he used to play catch with his friends, how he used to climb trees and how he would often annoy his teachers by playing pranks on them. He wished he could turn time and go back to those days when he didn't have to worry about getting the perfect job or the perfect bride.

He looked around. The entrance was decorated with flowers. There was a big banner with a picture of the classical danseuse Kiranmayi. She looked as beautiful as the flowers that were around her. Ravi couldn't help but smile.

There were directions that led Ravi to the playground. At the far end, there was a concrete stage where the show would take place. The crowd was slowly streaming in, some excited and some curious to see what they would experience. Some of the teenagers were already taking photos and recording videos for their social media. Ravi walked over to two empty chairs and sat on one of them. He placed his handkerchief on the other chair blocking it for Kiran and pulled out his phone.

Ravi dialled Kiran's number and waited. But Kiran's phone was unreachable. Ravi sent a WhatsApp message: "Come to the dance programme, if possible. The show is about to start," but there was no response. Kiran's "last seen" was turned off as well.

However, deep down, Ravi knew that Kiran might not show up because he did say he had some other work to attend. He sighed softly and looked around. The show would begin soon. He decided to record it for Kiran to show to him later on.

The chairs had been filled with cheerful and excited people. The kids ran around the playground while the parents tried to stop them. Staff members could be seen near the stage attending to last-minute arrangements.

Ravi's heart was beating excitedly. He only saw Kiranmayi on stage a few weeks before and impressed with her performance, he saw all her dance videos on YouTube. She had performed in various cities and events and word had it that Kiranmayi was hard to reach because of her busy schedule and appointments. Ravi felt as though the gods had answered his prayers because he wanted to see her perform live again and wanted to take her autograph. In fact, he wanted to initiate a conversation with her.

Kiranmayi's moves were like no other performer's. The way she danced, the way she played with her expressions felt like an exquisite piece of art, something that was rare and couldn't be judged or prejudiced.

As the sun was just on the horizon, the show began under the orange and purple sky. The host came up on the stage and said a few words about Kiranmayi, how she came from a small town and grew up to be such an amazing dancer.

Ravi clapped along with the audience. He braced himself as the lights on the stage went off for a bit. He waited for the dramatic moment when the lights would turn on and Kiranmayi would be on stage, posed in her signature pose before she prayed to the gods and began dancing.

The crowd turned quiet. Ravi amused himself with the thought that it was as if people were kids again and the principal had told them to stay quiet or stand out of the class. The lights turned on. The crowd cheered and gasped when they saw Kiranmayi standing on the stage, poised and looking as beautiful as the sun that was setting. Ravi had to raise his head high to see the dance as the people in front of him kept on raising their hands to clap loudly.

The music began and Kiranmayi started dancing. The crowd was pulled into an immersive experience, not even blinking lest they miss a crucial move in her performance or even an eye-contact. She wasn't an idol, but she was loved by her fans and that, Ravi thought, was more than enough for a performer. To be loved, to be heard, and to be seen.

Ravi was certainly mesmerised by Kiranmayi's dance. He was aware that she was an expert in performing different styles but watching her live was a whole new thing. He could feel his heart blooming and a sense of tranquillity seeping inside him.

Kiranmayi's performance was long but the more people watched her, the more they wished time would stop. Her eyes were wide and bold; darkened with *kohl*, her smile was like a painting; flawless and her arms and legs looked like delicate butterflies.

She performed several acts, starting with *Shiva Stuti* in *Kuchipudi*. It was an act where the dancer praised Lord Shiva and his relationship with Parvati. After that, she performed *Vighna Vinashkara* in *Vilasini Natyam*[25] which eulogised Lord Ganesh and lastly -- and the one which made the crowd give a standing ovation -- was *Adhyatma Ramayanam* in *Andhra Natyam*. This act presented the *Parashurama Garvabhanga Ghatam*.

"Who is she?" Ravi thought with awe. And she excelled in many forms of dance. Today, she performed *Kuchipudi, Vilasini Natyam*, and *Andhra Natyam*. Even the greatest dancer from their town, Sravanya, excelled in only one form. There weren't any coverage or interviews in the media about her personal life either. The more Ravi looked at Kiranmayi, the more he desired to meet her. He started planning on ways he could meet her and perhaps even shake her hands. *Should he buy her flowers first? But he wouldn't have time for that. Should he, maybe, buy her a box of chocolates*

---

[25] Indian classical dance. Its repertoire comprises temple dances, court dances, and dance operas of female singer-dancers of Telugu origin.

so that she can remember him always? All of these thoughts ran inside Ravi's head like a little kid chasing a balloon.

Ravi planned on how he would approach her: if he went behind the school, he could jump over the wall where it was broken and go to the staff room. Most probably that's the green room. To go behind the school, he could go out of the entry gate and walk around the compound wall. But it was risky. There would be the watchman, lights, vehicles, and people going back from the event as well as those still hanging out and talking. Someone would notice him, call him back or start talking. He glanced around thinking frantically. He spotted a hole in the wall away on the other side of the basketball court. The area there was not illuminated. He could squeeze through it and reach the back of the school.

"Yes, this is a good plan, I will be able to reach Kiranmayi," he said to himself.

*****

The show ended, Kiranmayi bowed to show her gratitude to the audience and left the stage. Ravi, needless to say, and everyone else present there, hoped for Kiranmayi to say a few words herself but she didn't. The crowd's murmur soon died as the host appeared on stage to thank everyone for coming to the show.

Many of them were already leaving or heading off to the stalls to buy Kiranmayi's dance video CDs and merchandise that had her face on it. Apparently, those items were only exclusive for this show as limited editions. However, as much as Ravi would have loved to buy any of those items, he decided to execute the plan he had plotted beforehand.

He was a bit wary that he could get caught as a peeping tom but when he thought about Kiranmayi and how he would finally get to see her face to face within inches from him, his anxiety died down and he could move his feet again. He looked around once to see if there were any watchmen around or not. Fortunately, the back of the school was as empty as a church on a weekday. Ravi reached the green room without any hitches.

He peeped through a window ledge and saw Kiranmayi standing in front of the mirror and looking at herself. Ravi's lips curled into a soft smile as he stared at the beauty in front of him. He still couldn't believe how someone could be so talented and beautiful at the same time.

Kiranmayi did look a bit tired. Beads of sweat were lingering on her forehead and her breathing was shallow. Doing three acts in one event did take a toll on a fragile body like Kiranmayi.

Ravi wished he could offer her something chilled to drink but he would rather watch her from afar than get caught by her and sent away. He never thought he would do something like this but here he was staring at her as though she was a portrait in a gallery.

She sat on the chair and began to remove her *ghungroo* and her jewelry. It took her awhile to remove the flowers as well from her hair and even the wig which looked as heavy as lead.

Kiranmayi then briskly wiped her make-up with wet wipes; starting from her eyes and then going down all the way to the neck. She had to use a few more wet wipes to take off the layers of her make-up. Once she was done, she threw the tissues into the trash can and sighed as she leaned back on her chair and looked into the mirror. Ravi's eyes were wide, and his hands trembled as he stared at the face, the same face, but now looking different.

He stared at his best friend.

*****

Kiran changed into his usual T-shirt and jeans, removing all accessories that of a woman. He then grabbed his back-pack and stealthily stepped out from the green room.

Ravi came out of his shock. He wasn't going to let this slide and hastened towards the door.

Just as Kiran stepped out, he was taken aback to see Ravi with his eyes wide with rage and hands on his hips. Ravi gritted his teeth and grabbed Kiran's collar. Before Ravi could say anything, Kiran unclasped Ravi's hands and rushed him back to the school compound wall where it was dark and nobody around.

Kiran inhaled deeply and looked at Ravi with gentle but glazed eyes. "Please… I will explain everything to you," he said.

Ravi stood up straighter and glared at Kiran. "You lead a double life! Never have you told me about it and you call yourself my best friend?"

Ravi's anger was scarier than an angry bull, but Kiran knew that if he was honest then Ravi would try and understand the situation he was in. "I know and I'm sorry Ravi but it's awfully difficult for me to lead the life of a male dancer."

Ravi scoffed and crossed his arms. "Don't divert the discussion Kiran."

"I'm not. You should know Ravi that I lived in the fear of being judged and my prospects harmed." Kiran's voice was shaky as he tried to hold back his tears. He didn't want to hide his true identity, but he had no choice.

Ravi sighed and shook his head. "Listen. I do know that there are difficulties in every trade and every profession but what I'm pissed off about is that you did not trust me enough to tell me that you were Kiranmayi, the most amazing and beautiful dancer out there!"

Kiran swallowed a heavy lump in his throat. "You are my best friend Ravi. I have my bike here in the bushes behind the wall. You must have parked your bike in the front gate, right?"

Ravi nodded slowly.

"Go back the way you came here and we will talk tomorrow."

Kiran was tired and he needed some time for himself after such a hectic event. He walked into the dark as Ravi, who was still seething with anger and hurt pride, headed towards the school gate while mumbling to himself about the injustice he received from Kiran.

*****

That night Sadanand Sastri was late for home. He sat in the temple's office working on some account ledgers. He was embezzling the temple cash but tying up the accounts was hard work. And to add to his problems, the village chief, Parasuram, applied for a grant from the State Board. And if the State Board approved his application, it meant all the temple's accounts would be audited, and the money that he had been pilfering would be no more a secret. He would not only be an outcast from the temple but also from his community. No one would call him to offer *pujas* and not to mention the shame and embarrassment he and his family would suffer.

All these days he was the king. The thought of shame and public humiliation took his sleep away. And so he started to insert false figures in the ledgers to tie up the missing cash. Pleased by his false figures, he locked the office behind him and stepped into the cold night. He wrapped his saffron shawl tighter around his body slowly walking out of the temple premises.

Was it an orange tail? Was it a flaming snake?

He was not sure. He rubbed his eyes and squinted into the dark. There was nothing there. An owl hooted somewhere. He was definitely hallucinating. But tonight, he would sleep. He had accounted for most of the missing cash in the books by showing false repairs and expenses.

A flaming snake.

He saw it again. He wasn't hallucinating. The hairs on his neck stood in terror. He felt goosebumps on his legs and hands. In that state of confusion, the orange shawl flew into the wind. He turned and hurried for the temple gate. Taking refuge in the temple was the best option. He would sleep in the temple the whole night, bad and evil spirits could not step inside the temple even if they wanted to. He would be safe there. He trotted towards the temple, retracing back on the path he had walked so far. He heard a swift swish in his ears.

Must be the wind.

He started to jog. He heard a long hiss as if a snake had whispered into one of his ears.

Must be the wind.

He ran without looking back and felt slightly relieved when the temple gate came into his vision. He increased his speed and just as there were a few feet between him and the gate, lights flickered vigorously. On...Off...On...Off. He stood there watching the on and off, his brain muted, his body rigid and fixed on that spot.

There was a hiss from behind which became a loud buzz in his ears and before he could realise, the on and off in front of him became a raging snake of light. Even before his brain reacted, the raging snake of light became shards of light and pierced him from all directions. The buzz in his ears died down, he felt something hot entering his ears, the buzzing sound was now coming from inside his body. He looked at his stomach, blood dripping out of the holes the shards of light had made. Before he could realise what was happening to him, a bunch of fireflies that were inside him escaped through his eyes burning his eyes and melting his eyeballs.

His horrid scream filled the night followed by a loud thud. Sadanand Sastri died a few inches away from the temple gate, his body pierced with many shards, his eyes burned out, and as the finishing touch, the fireflies charred the area of his forehead where there were three lines in white *Vibhuti* now replaced by three thick burnt lines of flesh.

Chapter - 8

Kiran waited for his friend in the parking area. He should have been here by now. He called Ravi but no answer. This was the third time he called. It was already 9.30. He was late for the first time since he started working here. Dejected, he directly went to his desk without having breakfast. If this was his friend's way of punishing him, he was okay with the terms. And if going without food could win over his friend back, he would go without food for the next two days as well.

Just pick up my call, please!

He tried again after an hour, no response. Work was not getting done either.

"Everything alright?" Sarma sir asked him. Kiran gave a quick nod.

"There was another grotesque murder, last night. Do you know who was killed?" Sarma Sir asked Kiran who shook his head slowly, fear and anxiety gripping him within.

"The head priest, Sadanand Sastri. Someone murdered him very cruelly just inches away from the temple gate." Sarma Sir removed his glasses and wiped them.

Kiran felt relieved. He was so worried about Ravi. Sarma Sir put his glasses back, "Kiran, he was my friend." There was a tinge of loss in his voice.

Kiran understood more than anyone how he felt. "Sir, why don't you take leave today?"

Sarma Sir nodded, went to the manager's cabin to ask for approval, collected his bag and lunchbox and left the office.

Kiran then went to speak to his manager. Seeing him enter the cabin, Ashok Kumar said in a sad tone, "What's happening to our town, Kiran? The priest is dead now. His body was found in the morning hours."

"I heard. Do you know whether Ravi is on leave today?" Kiran tried to sound flat as if he was asking casually.

"What happened? You guys had a fight? Ravi called me early in the morning today and said his *pinni* (aunty) is not well. He wants to visit her in Hyderabad and will be on leave this week."

"I see." Kiran spoke as if it was a whisper.

Walking out of the boss's cabin, his tensed muscles relaxed. He was okay with his friend being angry with him. He deserved this treatment from him. He should have told the truth to him before. He should have told his best friend a long time ago about his dual life. But he was afraid. He was neck deep in his greyness that he could not see the bright light at the end of the tunnel.

His friend was his light, his confidant, the only other person in this entire world who cared about him other than his mother. His father too cared about his son but in his own way. And if his father learnt that he danced beautifully when he decided to dance in a female form, his father would hang himself to save himself from the embarrassment of being called as the father of a queer. His father accepted him as a dancer after a long struggle, he did not want to worsen his relationship further with his father.

At the same time, sometimes it felt right for him to dance in a woman's form because he thought he brought justice to the character. And it was his choice, isn't it? To dance like Lord Shiva or the Goddess Parvati? Why should the world judge him? And why should he prove his sexual orientation all the time.

Settling in his chair, he looked through the window, watching the mango leaves fluttering to the afternoon breeze. At least, some things were not complex. They were simple to comprehend. Like the leaves dancing to the wind, the sun rising and setting, fireflies glowing. He hummed his favourite song to engage his mind, "The fireflies stole my light…"

The fireflies stole my light
and turned me into a dark night.
I walk in long tunnels
My heart in shambles,
Don't take me for a fool,
I am stuck in a litter-pool.
I met one of my old pals
Like me, he too lost his balls
I plead him to catch that fly
and kill it on a sly.
I want my light back
To return to my pack.
We sat in a bar drinking wine
Hoping all will be fine
But the night grew dark
And I remained a lone lark.
The fireflies stole my light
and turned me into a dark night.
My pal lent me some of his light
but I paid him back with a fist fight
The real ruin started now
You reap what you sow
I want to trap it in a jar
And see it die from afar.
I went in search of it
But I was tricked neat
I lost the battle very cheap
two cents and the price of a soap.
My buddy gave his hand
and pulled me out of the death-sand.
A new life, a new beginning
the old saga I won't be singing
Let the fireflies have my light
I found a friend who will do me right
If I have to cut a deal ever
I will choose my friend forever.
Let the fireflies have my light

There is a morning after every night.

*****

A small crowd of journalists had gathered outside the police station when Sravanya and Parasuram arrived there. Bangaru Babu stood outside at the entrance and tried to collect some gossip from the journalists. Inside, the fat SI chewed on the betelnut. Seeing Sravanya and Parasuram, he said, "We are waiting for the official autopsy report on Sadanand Sastri's death."

Sravanya nodded as Parasuram pulled the chair for her to sit across the table facing the SI. "We heard some disturbing facts on the news about the way he was murdered. How much of it is true?"

SI Suresh Pidugu with his mouth full of saliva ready to be spit out spoke, irritating Sravanya in the process, "The eyes were burnt out. The eardrums were also destroyed. And there were many piercings on his body. We think that death was primarily because of the numerous piercings in his body by a sharp object like shards of glass. Looks like someone stabbed with some sharp shards repeatedly over and over."

Sravanya and Parasuram were lost in their thoughts for a few moments.

"Why were the eyes burnt out and not the entire body? How can just one part of the body be burnt out without the rest of the body?" Sravanya questioned.

"In the first case, the victim had burnt marks and the medical officer couldn't identify why the internal parts of the body were burnt out, but the exterior remained intact," Parasuram added.

The SI simply nodded. He got up and went out of the room. When he came back his mouth was empty. Sravanya thought at least the guy can speak clearly now and she did not have to hear the chewing sound.

Adjusting his belt, he took his seat, "It seems there was some problem between you and the priest." The SI gave a sharp look at Parasuram.

"As Sravanya mentioned last time, he opposed our proposal for making the fort and temple a bigger tourist destination," Parasuram explained.

"Why would he oppose?"

Parasuram shrugged.

"Sir, did you do a thorough search of the fort? Maybe you would find a clue there." Sravanya asked with hope of getting some information.

"We did Madam. I sent out a team yesterday and I personally supervised the search. But we did not find anything."

"Did you also canvas the area behind the fort? There is a lot of ground there," Parasuram asked with renewed inquisitiveness.

"You seem to know that area well. How?"

"I took a land engineer to measure the surrounding area so that we could add all those details in our proposal. There is a cave beyond the fort. Did your team go there?"

"The cave is mostly ruined. Has a very small opening. There is nothing inside the cave. Just darkness and dead shrubs. That's all. But we found footprints which matched the dead student. Looks like he was in the cave and ran out from there; and somewhere in between the fort and the cave, he was attacked and killed." The SI spoke as if he has found a vital clue.

"I think, Inspector, you should canvas the area at night. Some things walk this earth only at night."

The inspector raised his eyebrows.

Sravanya got up, "Mamayya, we should go now. We should let Suresh Sir do his work."

Once they were out, Parasuram asked, "Why did you stop me?"

"Do you think he would have believed you?"

Bangaru Babu stopped them, "Let us go from the back door. There is a big crowd of journalists. And they will pounce upon you for interviews.

Back in the car, Parasuram sighed, "That was a relief not answering the press questions." Bangaru Babu was also Parasuram's driver. As he drove the car out of the police station, Bangaru Babu opened the conversation, "Last night I met Raju at our usual hide-out, the small bar where we all usually gather. Raju sounded gibberish to me, he was talking about some lights being on and off, strange lights flickering over the fort on the night he took the college students to the fort. He did not make any sense to me. But it looks like he saw something. Mamayya, shall I call him to meet you in the evening? You might understand what he is trying to tell."

"Sure. Why not? We must collect all the information we can get. But the strange lights he is talking about could be fireflies. That area has a lot of fireflies."

"But Mamayya, he was also talking about some watchers."

"The cave, to me, looks like the power centre of..." He trailed off not knowing what to call it.

"Ghost," Bangaru Babu offered.

"There are no ghosts," Sravanya said firmly.

"Then explain how someone was able to burn out a few body parts?" Parasuram questioned her.

"Some chemical or something."

"Which chemical melts the eyes like that. Must be acid. And why isn't the area around the eyes not burnt? You heard the inspector say it is only the eyes and the ears. And in the previous murder, it was the food pipe, and parts of stomach. So, um," Parasuram was trying to find words.

"Are you trying to imply that something entered these people through their nose or ears or mouth and burnt them from inside?"

Bangaru Babu stared at Sravanya in horror through the rear-view mirror.

"Yes. That could be the only explanation. But what are these? Some insects or bugs?"

"Your theory is weird, Mamayya." Sravanya rubbed her temples, a mild headache had started.

"You don't believe me? I will prove my theory to you, Sravanya. Bangaru Babu, Raju, and I will be on a stake out at the fort tonight. We will observe if some strange things happen there. And the lights that Raju blabbered about, let's see if we can see some." Parasuram seemed happy at his plan.

He removed the old diary from his bag and showed a page scribbled in neat handwriting to Sravanya. She read out those lines loud, "The transgender was buried in the deserted cave behind the fort. Only the soldiers of the *poligar* knew where they had buried him. They did it in the silence of the night. The priest was happy. All of them could now peacefully restore to their debauchery acts in the name of God and *devadasis*. The India I have come to know is also the land of hypocrisy - I have seen a great deal of sexual exploitation carried out in the shadows." It was signed by Sir Malcom and dated as 24th June, but the year was not mentioned. Definitely the pre independence era but which year was not clear.

"Let's say it is the ghost of this transgender."

"Bhushan."

"Okay. Bhushan. But why was he silent all these years?"

"I don't know. We have to find the answers. Until we find the answers to all the questions, I am afraid we can't fight against it. And we have to find them fast. I can't just sit idle and watch Bhushan murder innocent people."

They waited in the car at the foot of the steps keeping a watch on the fort. Parasuram wanted to go up but Raju was too afraid to go. He accompanied them on one condition that they won't go up and that too in the night. Reluctantly, Parasuram agreed. Three were better than two. How? He didn't understand. He just thought the more the better and if that more was just one person more.

"You see them, they are watchers. They watch everyone. They are like the soldiers of the fort." Raju spoke in a very low tone as if the watchers would listen to him.

"They are just boulders." Bangaru Babu patted on his back. But Raju was not convinced.

"What did you see that evening, exactly?" Parasuram asked, stepping out of the car drawing some fresh air and stretching his legs. "So far it is all silent here. But something about the vibe this area is giving, I don't feel good. I have this constant nag in my head that something is lurking in the darkness."

"Yes. I always have that creepy feeling when I am here. That's why I don't go up. It is creepier up there. I feel my insides getting twisted."

Bangaru Babu flinched at Raju's description. Sitting in the driver's seat, he looked around. There was darkness all around except the few spaces where the car's front and back lights threw light. It was a starry night. The moon was almost full. Bangaru Babu was thankful for the full moon.

The negative vibe that Mamayya and Raju were talking about, he did not understand that. But he looked at those boulders again in the moonlight, and they did look like hooded men staring at them. He smiled. How the light was at different angles and the way the boulders were placed made them look like hooded faces. He smiled thinking of Raju's description about them. He hoped the lights too were a trick played by the stars.

In the distance, on the top of the hill, just over the boulders, he saw a strange flicker of lights. He touched Raju's shoulder who was sitting next to him. Raju looked at where Bangaru Babu was staring. His eyes widened and his mouth opened. Parasuram was pacing around the car with his hands at his back.

"Mamayya, LOOK!" Bangaru called out to him. Parasuram turned his head to the fort, and within that second, a huge swarm of glowing bees marched in a vehement attack. In the dark, these glowing bugs formed a shape of a dragon and approached them at tremendous speed. On the line of attack from these creatures, God only knew what they were, panic hit them numbing their brain for a split second.

Bangaru Babu screamed, "Mamayya, get inside." Parasuram ran quickly to get inside the car. He was a few steps away from the car. The speed at which the glowing dragon was approaching, Bangaru Babu feared whether Parasuram could make it. Raju and he started to wind up the windows of the car. This was an old Maruti 800 and the windows had to be wound up.

Parasuram quickly jumped into the back seat and wound the glass escaping from the glowing bugs by a hairline. Some of the glowing bugs bumped against the car windowpane and fell down. They were crushed by bumping against the glass, but they did not bleed. They fell down. It was a big swarm, and millions of those glowing creatures dashed against all the glasses. Luckily, the other side of the windowpane was already closed by Raju before Parasuram got in. They all watched in muted terror at those bugs dashing against their car windows in a constant barrage. All of them were scared to utter a single word. They waited for the lighting bugs to give up. Realizing that they cannot get in, they retreated.

"Are they gone?" Raju asked, still holding his breath.

"I think so," Bangaru Babu answered. Both looked around through the windows.

"What should we do now?"

"Let's go. We cannot fight them anyway. But I have found a few answers." Parasuram stuttered to speak the words.

Raju started the engine. It made a heavy creaking sound and died down. He tried again. But the engine did not start.

"God! We are struck," Raju yelped in fear.

"The car was fine. I don't know why it would not start. I will get down and take a look at it. The fireflies are gone, I believe," Bangaru Babu suggested.

"No. You will not get down. What if they waited so that one of us gets down and they can attack us?"

Raju started at Parasuram words, shivering all over. Large beads of sweat fell down from his face.

"Those were just swarms of bees. They are not that intelligent to hunt us." Raju looked back at Parasuram.

"Babu, they are not just swarms of bugs. They are controlled by some higher force. Did you not observe their coordinated movement? And when I was getting into the car, I could feel their heat. These were the bugs that burnt the victims."

Raju was so terrified that he could not speak a single word. Bangaru Babu, on hearing Parasuram's deduction, felt like retching, imagining the fireflies entering into his mouth. "But what I don't understand is how the car's engine is dead? Unless…," he stopped at his thought.

"Yes. I am also thinking the same. They might have entered inside the car's engine through the exhaust nozzle and the engine could not start because something is stuck in one of its pipes." Parasuram was also frightened. He did not remember any incident from his life when he was frightened so much.

"Do you think we are safe in the car?" Raju spoke in a trembling voice.

"I think so. Let's wait in the car till morning. I think they do not have powers during the day."

So they waited for the sun to rise, listening to the loud heartbeats of each other and to their heavy breathing. After a while, it looked like the fireflies had abandoned them, but they did not want to take the risk. So they sat in the car sweating their brains and bodies until the first ray of the sun fell on them. Bangaru Babu had tried turning on the engine many times during the night but with no luck. The engine did not revive. He tried then again. The car did not start still.

Thinking it is safe to get down, Bangaru Babu and Raju got down, covering their face and ears. After some time, when they were sure they were safe, they removed the cloth from around the face and signalled Parasuram to step out.

Parasuram had expected a few dead bugs on the road, the ones that dashed against the windowpane, but there were none on the road. Raju opened the bonnet and checked the engine. But it did not start. They decided to leave the car and walk to the main road where they can get lift and get a mechanic down here or even get the car towed.

"We have to kill the fireflies. That's how we can stop the ghost. But how do we kill them?" Parasuram talked to himself as they walked. Raju and Bangaru Babu walking briskly and Parasuram following them lost in his thoughts.

"We can't kill them, but we can trap them into a jar or bottle" he answered himself.

While Parasuram and his small party were halted by the fireflies, Sravanya did a little research on ghosts and evil spirits but nothing was forthcoming.

Frustrated, she switched on the tape, and Yazaan's beautiful voice filled her room. He was singing in African, a lullaby he said it was. She closed her eyes, swayed away by the beautiful music. A sense of serenity swept her whole being and she went into the state of dreams. She sat on a bench watching a seagull flying over the river. The evening sun started to set. The river shimmered under the sun. She felt a warm touch on her shoulder. She turned to look back who it was. She couldn't see the face. It was a shadow. She asked, "Who are you?"

A voice came back, "A greater artist than you. I have come to teach you art that is primordial and eternal."

"And what is that?"

"Love - the greatest art of all."

Chapter - 9

Last night, Kiran cried himself to sleep. There were very few such situations in his life so much so that he could count on his fingers, and last night he added one more to the list. The day when his father ripped the skin off his back, the day when he was bullied in school for wearing a girl's costume and playing the female ballerina for a play, the day when his Guru found out that he lied about his caste to get admission into her class, and today, when his best friend wouldn't talk to him.

The sun rays illuminating the windows of his room disturbed him. He squinted his puffed eyes, got up from the bed and closed the window that must have opened because of the wind. Satisfied with his dark room, he dragged himself over to his bed, sent a message to his boss that he will be on leave. He did not feel like going to work. He did not feel like doing his dance practice today. He wanted to sleep without any of those negative thoughts running through in his head.

The whole night he blamed himself for not telling his friend. And then the whole night, that familiar cloud of insecurity rained on him. He hugged his pillow tight like a small child, his eyes vacant, and his mind trying to find a plausible explanation that he would give to his friend when he would be back. And how does he stand now in Ravi's eyes? That day in the canteen Ravi had judged him. Would he understand him now if he would even try to explain himself? He was wrong in hiding his dual life from his friend but why was he supposed to explain himself? Wasn't Ravi his best friend? And best friends don't run away.

For that one moment he was very angry at Ravi and wanted to punch him for avoiding him. Who was the bigger coward now? He was happy at least he had a best friend if not his love along his side. But as of that morning, he was back to his loneliness and his greyness, his one-sided love was never by his side and now his best friend too had left him. Tears welled up in his eyes. He pressed his face into the pillow as if that would reduce his pain. He slowly sank into a wave of nausea. He was elsewhere now.

He was sleeping on something solid, black. The softness of his bed and the pillow were gone. It took some time to realise that he was in the temple's outer podium where he had recently performed. It was here Ravi had seen Kiranmayi. Why did he even agree to do a performance here? He should have kept his performances out of this town. Bad decision. But he can't undo anything of that now.

It was evening time. There were no lights. He was alone on the stage. There was no audience. The sky looked a tinge of purple slowly mixing into the black shade. It would be night soon. The painting underneath him glowed in the dark. The luminous *Ardhanareeswara* smiled at him. But something was happening to it. The white paint was dripping down, and the entire painting became distorted in just a few seconds. He sat straight looking at the painting melting down in horror. The white paint that had dripped and flowed recklessly on the black stone started to fade.

He started to weep. His *Ardhanareeswara* was gone, what was left was some smudged white paint a few seconds before and now that too had disappeared. It was his favourite mural, something very precious in abstract to him, something he cherished in his soul, not the painting itself but what it portrayed. The sky turned dark. He wondered why there isn't one single star. Out of nowhere, lights flickered everywhere.

Fireflies!

At first there were very few, then some more, then hundreds, thousands and then millions of them. And all of them at once started to fly towards him. He held his breath in unknown fear, but the fireflies settled on the black podium in a pattern glowing vigorously, switching their light on and off. He stood up and saw the beautiful *Ardhanareeswara* formed by these radiant fireflies. And in their light, he forgot all his sadness, all his anguish, all his rage. He was the man and the woman in the painting.

The fireflies shifted a little and when the shifting stopped, the woman's face was of Sravanya. He sat down and touched the face gently, the gold of the fireflies shimmered on his hand. He slept on the figure created by the fireflies, the glowing *Ardhanareeswara*, spreading his arms wide open over them, his body illuminated by thousands of fireflies, his skin started to shed, the brown colour of his dermis turned gold, he was now one with the fireflies, he was one with the *Ardhanareeswara*. Kiran's body shifted over the bed, his legs and hands wide, sleeping over on his stomach, he smiled in his sleep.

The heat of the day seeped into her veins that was how she felt. And when dusk settled in, she realised that the foreign body creeping in her blood was "fear". But there was another thing that happened simultaneously in her nerves. A strange bug crawled there, she felt mild jolts and then a rush. She finally understood it – "adrenaline". A strange combination!

Who had thought that in this technological age, ghosts made cameo appearances once in a while? She imagined the scene of large swarms of fireflies attacking Mamayya and Bangaru Babu. It scared her. She knew what she imagined was not even a fraction of what they experienced. Parasuram had called her in the afternoon after reaching home and updated her regarding the recent events.

They decided to meet next morning to plan their next move. They all needed a good night's sleep to ponder on the idea that a ghost existed. But the big question was whether they could sleep knowing that killer bugs lurked out there in the dark waiting for an opportunity to kill them. The thought of this supernatural being spooked her. And at the same time, it created some sort of fire in her. The excitement of fighting against it was something she was unable to resist. The idea of becoming the Goddess and slaying the demon was already rooted in her mind. No matter what, with the help of Parasuram, Bangaru Babu and driver Raju, she was going to kill the ghost and free the town from its evil clutches.

But how does one kill something which was already killed? She decided to browse over the internet and hoped to gather some information that could help her team. As she started to browse, the unknown voice in her dream echoed in her ears. It had said, "I will teach you love." Who was that man? And the timing of the dream could not possibly be a coincidence? For now, the dream had to go in the back alleys of her mind.

"Why have you closed all the windows Sraavi?" Nanna stood at the doorway of her room, "It is so hot."

She didn't know what to tell. She didn't want to tell anything about the ghost or the attack on Mamayya. And why make her parents worry unnecessarily?

"Just like that. Please keep them closed. Switch on the AC if you like," she replied casually.

"Everything alright? Something we should know." Her father was worried. No matter how hard she tried, it was always difficult to keep anything away from her parents. They always got the nerve of the situation in some way or the other. But this was different.

"All okay. But please do not open the windows." She smiled trying to look calm and relaxed. Her father smiled and went away leaving her daughter to her browsing.

Dinner was neatly served by Bangaru Babu but Parasuram did not have the appetite to eat. Two plain curries and curd, simple food, but still his stomach did not have the capacity to digest plain food. The shock of the attack was still there, a bit faded, but it was there. The image of millions of golden bugs attacking him like thunder fire kept playing again and again in his mind. What would have happened if he would not have made it to the car and locked the windows? All those millions of bugs probably would have entered his mouth, and then his stomach. The thought made him puke. He pushed his plate showing his disapproval to eat.

"You must eat. You need the strength," Bangaru Babu insisted. Parasuram took small bites of food and ate with great difficulty. Lunch, of course, did not feel this way. They had gobbled it quickly and crashed on their beds. They were exhausted from the night and the long walk from the fort to the main road. Bangaru Babu was also shaken but he was stronger and younger than Parasuram. He managed his fears better.

After dinner, Bangaru Babu cleaned up and retired to his small room. He once again checked that all the windows of the house were closed. But he could not sleep. He was too scared to sleep. What if he was busy sleeping and those dreadful things entered his room and his nose or ears or eyes? His body jerked in fear and he sat upright. A sudden thought disturbed him.

He took a few towels and blankets from the cupboard and squeezed them in the opening between the door and the floor. What if the fireflies entered from there? He stuffed the towels in the main door, Parasuram's bedroom door and his door from inside. He was definitely acting paranoid. But better be safe than sorry, he assured himself. He called Raju and told him that he should be doing the same thing. Cover the space underneath the door with some cloth. Raju had gone a step further. He had bordered his bed with God's frames and if the ghost dared come close to him, the gods would rebuke the ghost. And Bangaru Babu thought he was the one who was overreacting.

Parasuram paced the room unable to sleep. He missed his wife Malati. At this moment, he needed her the most. He longed to hear the soothing words in her soft voice, "Don't worry Parasu, everything will be okay." And those words had a magic impact on him. He would regain his lost strength. In that quick moment he grabbed his mobile and called his wife's number, but he cut it off without the call going through. She must be asleep. He could call her tomorrow morning. And in one way it was good that she was not here. It was good that she went on a *Tirtha Yatra* with their friends. Parasuram was supposed to go with her but he cancelled the trip at the last minute because of the meeting with the Tourism Minister. He did not expect to get a meeting with the Tourism minister so quickly but Sravanya had pulled some of her contacts and a meeting found its way in the busy calendar of the chief minister.

Everything was going good as per their plan, but the murder of the tourist student followed by a series of murders had washed away the hard work they had put in to get the required sanctions and funds for developing the town into a better tourist spot and restoring the dilapidated fort and repairing the broken sections of the temple. He collapsed on his bed feeling the weight of the responsibility on his shoulders. Working up on a plan to stop Bhushan was the bigger problem, but there were incidental problems that needed diplomacy in handling them.

One problem was how much information should he share in the *panchayat* meeting to be held the next day? Now that Sadanand Sastri was no more, Seshadri was the chief priest. If handling Sadanand Sastri was difficult, handling Seshadri and talking some sense into his rigid and orthodox mind was impossible. He could inform everyone about Bhushan but that would only lead to chaos. And the press would blow it up accusing him of spreading superstitions. And how was all of that going to help them stop Bhushan? And what about the police? Are they even equipped to handle such a kind of state enemy?

No one knew what to do. He had reached out to an exorcist from the neighbouring town as per Raju's recommendation. It seemed a logical choice. It was absolutely okay to consult with a person who had experience in that area. And who other than an exorcist was an expert in expelling the ghost from his town. Raju said that Badrinath was also a *tantrik*, and an accomplished one in his field.

The first thing he did that afternoon after reaching home was plugging his phone to a charger and placing the call to Badrinath. There was no response so he called Sravanya and told her his night adventure with the fireflies. They both agreed that these creatures that looked like fireflies were not fireflies at all.

He remembered his words to Sravanya over the phone, "The fireflies are his soul and they are his spirit. If we kill them, we can paralyze Bhushan." He was not sure if what he said was right then but as he mulled over it during the day and at night, in his wakeful state and in his sleep, only those lines made sense to him.

Badrinath had called him soon after his call with Sravanya. Parasuram did not mention the entire incident but told him he sought his advice on an important matter, and it was urgent and that many lives were at stake. Badrinath promised to meet him the next morning. That was a relief. As soon as the *panchayat's* meeting was over, he and Sravanya along with Bangaru Babu would seek Badrinath's help in stopping Bhushan. He lay on his bed thinking of what he would speak in the *panchayat's* meeting. He was grateful to Badrinath for helping them out and counted on his help thereby looking forward to the next day.

But what he didn't know was that the counsel on whom he was relying so heavily wouldn't be there at all by the time the sun rose.

Badrinath decided to travel that evening itself instead of waiting for the next day. He would stay at his cousin's place in Kotagiri for the night and meet the village head the next morning. Parasuram wouldn't have called him if it was not urgent. He was also sure that the call from the village head was something to do with the serial killings. He had to cross the fort to reach the town. But he was the *tantrik* and all the ghosts feared him. So he really did not think much of the sinister fort. And he had travelled many times on that path before. But that was before the murders.

But still, he was a tantrik and ghosts were scared of him.

He got a little delayed on the way due to an accident and by the time he was on the road next to the fort, it was a little over 7 pm He was driving his bike at 60 km per hour, and he had just crossed the fort. He saw huge flashlights in front of him like that of the headlights of a truck. And the truck was directly coming onto him. He honked but the truck did not move to right or left. It was heading straight towards him. He swerved a little to the right out of the truck's way on the road and the sudden swerve caused him to lose his balance. He tripped and the motorbike skidded, and he fell down a little afar, away from the road while the bike swept a little more on the *kacha* road and halted.

His knees were grazed and his hands cut from the impact. He stood up and walked slowly towards the bike cursing the truck. Where was the damn truck by the way? He did not hear the truck's engine. It was only the flashlights. He was thinking over what had just happened and at that moment a bug entered into his nose. He sneezed loudly and rubbed his nose. There was something in his ears and suddenly he felt a rush of something entering his nose and ears.

Before he could understand anything, he felt something moving in his throat that glowed in the dark of the night. Eyes wide he looked at it and the glow went off and suddenly his stomach glowed. He was wearing a black dhoti and a black shawl. The shawl had fallen off on the road when he was tossed to the side. He looked at his naked stomach glowing brightly in the dark, and before he knew what was happening a million light bugs burst out of his stomach throwing all his insides out. He collapsed on the ground.

His last thought was: *He was the greatest tantrik and ghosts were scared of him.*

Chapter - 10

The whole world swayed like a big black snake momentarily in front of his eyes. And everything came back in the form of lights blinking rhythmically, just like the ones he had seen over the fort two nights before. Parasuram was at the community hall in a *panchayat* meeting when Inspector Suresh Pidugu walked in the midst of the meeting and questioned him, "What was your business with *Tantrik* Badrinath? His wife told us that you called him to meet you urgently?" Parasuram was still recovering from the shock of Badrinath's murder. The meeting had a full quorum today. All the Temple Committee members, *panchayat* members and the rich and powerful men from the town were present. A low murmur that started between the attendees became a loud garble within seconds.

"Shshshsh!" The inspector shouted.

"I wanted his help to see if there is an evil spirit that is behind the murders." Parasuram finally spoke, coming out of the shock, the blinking lights in front of his eyes now gone. He had pinned his hopes on the exorcist and Bhushan murdered the exorcist. To whom should they turn for help now?

The low murmur was stirred again by the mention of the evil spirit among the crowd.

"I have been telling this from the day Sadanand Sastri was murdered. Parasuram, you did not heed to my advice, and now, we have one more murder. I told you that day itself we should be doing *yagnas*[26] and *pujas* to drive the evil spirit away from our town." Priest Seshadri spoke in a harsh and blaming voice.

"No, I did not ignore your advice. I needed more time to think," Parasuram explained.

But Seshadri was in no mood to listen. He was like that - stiff and adamant. "And see now, what happened? And why do you have to contact a *tantrik* from the neighbouring town, he is not even from our caste. You don't think we are capable enough?" Seshadri was furious now as if everything was because of Parasuram.

And that was the exact reason why Parasuram did not want to discuss or seek help from these elitist priests who always brought caste into the picture. He felt drained but he had to speak, "Look Seshadri, keep caste out of this entire thing. Badrinath was highly recommended to me by someone whom I knew for years. And what's wrong in asking help from our neighbours or from people from a different caste. And who am I to give you permission to perform *yagnas* or *homams* in the temple. If the temple committee deems it fit, please go ahead with the *yagnas*." Parasuram tried to handle the situation but Seshadri, the adamant fellow he was, simply indulged in blame game and started speaking of how they needed a more dynamic leader and that Parasuram no longer fit the bill. The real reason was that Seshadri's pride was hurt and he had expected that Parasuram would ask his advice and not that of Badrinath who belonged to a scheduled caste.

Inspector Suresh was annoyed at the internal politics. He had a serial murder to solve and these people were fighting over petty things. He asked them to finish the argument and asked more questions to Parasuram and Seshadri. "You people think there is an evil spirit...do you mean a ghost?"

Parasuram quickly answered before Suresh went further, "No, what I meant was just the evil eye."

---

[26] A Hindu ritual performed in which Agni Deva, the fire God acts as a medium between man and the gods.

But Seshadri did not like that, "Yes. There is an evil ghost in the town. We have to cleanse the town and eradicate it from here."

"So, who benefits by spreading such rumours?" Inspector Suresh asked Seshadri who shrugged his shoulders.

Suresh answered his question, "Naturally, the temple committee members."

Seshadri was enraged at the suggestion, "You inspector are a fool. You do what you have to do, and we will do what we have to do." He signalled his followers, "Let's go. We have to prepare for the *Maha Yagna*." All of them left except the SI, two constables, Parasuram, Bangaru Babu, Sravanya and two elderly people, a retired doctor and the headmaster of the government school.

Sravanya then asked the inspector, "Can we announce a lockdown until the murderer is caught."

The retired doctor nodded. The headmaster added, "We can take the help of local TV Channels and urge people to be cautious."

Sravanya saw an excellent opportunity and added, "And also lock their doors and windows after 6 pm."

"Yes. Why not? I will talk to the news channels." Inspector Suresh nodded and took leave.

The headmaster and the doctor also left. Parasuram collapsed on a chair with his face buried in his hands.

Sravanya sent Bangaru Babu to fetch *goli* soda[27] for all three of them. She sat on the adjacent chair and spoke gently, "Mamayya, don't be dejected. We will work out something."

"Sravanya, we should have acted soon." He spoke with his face buried in his hands.

---

[27] A colloquial term for carbonated lemon in a Codd-neck bottle popular in India.

"What do you think we should do next?" Sravanya asked.

Parasuram slowly turned his face, "We should go to the fort."

"Why? Do you think the killings are related to the fort?" Subramanyam, the journalist from *Andhra Velugu* newspaper walked in with a camera in his hand eager to know more.

Sravanya and Parasuram looked at each other and sighed.

"We were just discussing that the police should take another look at the road. It was mostly deserted, and someone could have waited there to kill Badrinath knowing that he was enroute to meet Parasuram Sir." Sravanya offered.

"Thank God I caught you two here while others ambled around Seshadri. I know that man cannot talk sensible things. Pure waste of time." He smiled but neither Sravanya nor Parasuram smiled back.

"Mamayya, do you really believe in the evil spirit that Seshadri has been babbling about?" He looked sharply at Mamayya.

"Subramanyam, you ask him. He was the one who kept on talking about the evil spirit and *yagnas* and all that stuff."

"He is just calling it evil spirit because he can't explain. And say, if really there is an evil spirit, what is its name? What is its story? And why is it killing people? Don't you think we need all these answers as well?" Both of them nodded.
"Was there any particular reason that you reached out to the *tantrik*?" Parasuram shook his head.

"The *tantrik* was murdered ruthlessly; his body parts were mangled..." Subramanyam wanted to say more but since Sravanya was there, he did not indulge more in the gory talk. Sravanya understood that when he fell silent in the middle of his talk. And that was one thing she never understood. Why do men always have to think that women didn't have the stomach to hear about the gore and evil things when a huge percentage of her tribe were actually suffering a lot crueller infliction?

"The police do not have a lead, but as a village head what do you think about this psycho killer who enjoys torturing his kill?"

"I can't say anything. But we have advised the SI to have a lockdown after 6 pm. We have also advised that people should lock their doors and windows after 6 pm, just to be extra cautious."

"That sounds best for now. But how does the lockdown or a *mahapuja* help to catch the killer. The casualties may be reduced because of the lockdown, the killer might not get a very easy opportunity, but how is it helpful to catch the killer?"

"Maybe the killer's desperation will force him to commit a mistake." Sravanya jumped in.

"Subramanyam, I hope you got your answers. I am really not in the mood to talk right now. Can you please excuse us?" Subramanyam nodded and walked out as Bangaru Babu came in with two soda bottles.

"Where is Raju?" Parasuram asked.

"He fled the town. He is terrified by the murder of the *tantrik*. He told me that if the *tantrik* cannot save himself from the ghost, and he is the greatest *tantrik*, how should he, a simple driver save his life."

"I don't blame him. It is natural to be scared." Parasuram slurped the cold soda, his throat felt better, his stomach cooled as the soda travelled from his throat to down below to his stomach but the thought of the *tantrik's* stomach strewn on the road made him puke.

They moved to a smaller room of the community hall in the back so that no one overheard them. Sravanya started the conversation, "I was reading the diary again. It talked about Bhushan wanting to become a *devadasi* but was rejected because he was a man."

Parasuram nodded and Bangaru Babu looked confused. "You mean a transgender?" He looked for clarification.

Sravanya gave a slight nod. "But nothing there explains about the fireflies or the light bugs you guys saw. I was doing a little research on fireflies last night and they are harmless. They don't even sting."

"If you look at it through the eyes of science, nothing makes sense but then all of this did happen, right?" Parasuram shifted a little in his seat, he closed his eyes for a minute and continued to talk as if he wanted a moment of clarity on what was going in his mind, "I think that all these years, must be approximately hundred, a year here or there, the soul of Bhushan became stronger and stronger. So strong that his soul manifests in the form of fireflies. All his soul energy, somehow, he was able to turn into those lightning bugs. And that's why or how I think he controls them; and if we kill the fireflies, we can paralyze his power."

"What if you are wrong?" Bangaru Babu furrowed with his eyebrows.

"You have a better theory? The exorcist who could have confirmed my theory or would have come up with a better one is dead," Parasuram grunted.

He leaned a little forward and looked directly into Sravanya's eyes, "*Thalli* (daughter), you know that I consider you as my daughter? And believe me, as a father, it is difficult to involve his own daughter in a war but then a father also knows, better be his own daughter at risk than any other girl. Will you help us in this mission?"

"Mamayya, it's an honour."

*****

The fort was unusually calm; there wasn't even the slightest breeze that evening. The sun did not set yet. It was just about twilight. They entered the cave shuddering with fear. It was unusually calm too. The light from outside lit the cave at its mouth and a few feet beyond. The three of them entered through the narrow opening. Bangaru Babu switched the huge flashlight he brought with him and kept it at a distance where the light from the opening of the cave did not reach. It lit the area beyond the light. There was a dead shrub. There were no fireflies. They focused on their hearing senses but there was no buzzing or hissing or swishing.

Dusk started to fill in. And they had to carry out their plan at the right time. If they waited too long, it would be night and his powers would be at the peak. Dusk was the time when he was not that powerful. Their plan was simple, and they were determined to perform their parts to the T in muted diligence.

Bangaru Babu switched on the tape. Sravanya did her *Namaskaram*. They kept another high voltage flash bulb in another corner. Sravanya was ready to perform *Tarangam*. A slow *alaap* reverberated in the cave slowly rising and then closing in a high pitch. Dressed in a yellow *sari* and pearl jewellery, she kept a mud pot and brass plate on her right side so that when the time was right, she would use them as her props in dance.

She tied her *ghungroo* as the *alaap* stopped and the *tabla* beats from the tape echoed in her ears like a war cry. A small lump had formed in her stomach and slowly the lump started to increase in its size reaching to her throat. For a brief moment, she could not breathe. This was not the time to be numb with fear. This was the time for action. This was the time to invoke her inner goddess, her soul energy, the *shakti* and slay a demon. The Goddess was with her today, the Goddess was within her. She had to strike that chord through her dance.

Taking long breaths, her legs and hands started to make movements at the *talam* from the tape. Her face was frozen, and her facial movements were dull and pale. Parasuram and Bangaru Babu had moved to a corner keeping a watch on the cave. Though the cave was calm, there was a strange feeling. Their guts were telling them that there was something weird there, but they could not actually lay a finger on it. Slowly, Parasuram realised what it was. It was a fourth breathing. All this while, there was another being in the cave, invisible but present. There weren't any eyes or any shadow or any animal or a bug but there was this strange feeling that there was someone else too.

Bangaru Babu also had the same feeling but more like how Raju had described - the insides being twisted. Bangaru Babu thought he was going to have a paralytic attack. But his fingers and feet were moving just fine. He closed his palms and opened them just to be sure. He wondered what *Akka* (sister) was thinking. As of now, she was doing great, she was performing very well. Even her facial muscles relaxed then. Her one leg was in the air and then on the ground. She danced on her toes and took quick rounds; her *ghungroo* tapped a rhythmic beat that felt soothing and serene in that ghastly cave. His setting up the camera on a tripod was done and everything was being recorded. The camera was for a dual purpose, to fool the ghost and to click the ghost. They wanted to trick the ghost that they were shooting a dance video and they wanted to catch the fireflies in action on camera. But the wicked could not be tricked that easy. And yet all complex problems in life had simple solutions if one tried to solve them step by step. This was what Parasuram believed. Bangaru Babu clutched the Hanuman locket tightly in his neck praying to the Almighty.

Sravanya completed her first act. She then stood up on the earthen pot and danced to the song from the tape. In this dance variation of *Kuchipudi*, the hand movements were heavy, and the emphasis was more on the facial expressions and the eye movement of the dancer. It was a brief act, but she had to bring the pot in her dance as naturally as possible. So far she was successful. But where were the fireflies? Didn't he like her dance? But how could he not like the dance? Was the rhythm too slow? Didn't she select a proper act? All types of questions filled her mind making her anxious.

She was about to lose her balance and trip from the pot, but she gained control. Just at the time that she was dejected and crestfallen, she saw a light flicker. Parasuram put his hand on Bangaru Babu's shoulder expressing it was time. Raw fear gripped them both. Parasuram felt like puking but he controlled himself. Bangaru Babu felt his muscles tightening in his stomach, he was going to have a paralytic attack soon, he thought. And Sravanya thought her heart came into her mouth. But she continued to dance on the pot, her hand and head movements unwavering in their precision.

The fireflies grew more as if they doubled, tripled, and quadrupled from one source and at a very fast rate. The blinking now became vigorous and the cave lit up golden in their bright light. The fear increased her heartbeat, and she was scared that they would come near to her. They didn't. They just blinked. The song on the tape came to a halt. A brief pause. She stood up on the brass plate and took the pot on her head. It was now time for the final act. With her legs placed stiff on the brass plate, she moved the plate on the new beat of the song from the tape.

First to right, then to left. She balanced the pot perfectly on her head without dropping it down. The fireflies that were scattered in the cave gathered at one spot, a few feet from Sravanya but facing her. Seeing all the fireflies gathered at one place in incandescent blaze steadily, Sravanya felt her blood pressure drop and thought she would faint. The familiar creeping and crawling in her nerves and veins made her miss a beat, but she gathered herself and caught up to the next beat.

The fireflies now lined up like a long wire of lights and slowly formed into two hands in *Namaskar*. Sravanya paused for a second not knowing what they were up to. Nevertheless, she continued to dance, her heart racing and her brain passive with fear. The hands (that the fireflies had formed into) started to imitate her. They copied her movements. They did exactly what she was doing.

Thakita Thom thak Thom thak dhirana
Kanaka mani mayi nopura charana
She kept her hands on her hips and moved the plate with her legs in the same Talam and ragam.

Thakita Thom thak Thom thak dhirana
Kanaka mani mayi nopura charana
The fireflies too moved and blinked their light in the same *talam* and *ragam* just like how music graphs showed on CD players and computers.

Thakita Thom thak Thom thak dhirana
Kanaka mani mayi nopura charana
She now took a complete round on the brass plate balancing the pot.
The fireflies too rotated around her encircling her blinking in a musical graph.

Bangaru Babu was worried and started to stand up but the firm hand of Parasuram on his shoulder stopped him.

Thakita Thom thak Thom thak dhirana
Kanaka mani mayi nopura charana

Sravanya went back on the brass plate in swift movements, her *ghungroo* and the sound of the plate matching the beat and music of the song. The fireflies too marched according to the tune blinking magically. She took the pot from her head and changed it from one side to the other side as the song went on playing in the tape. The fireflies mimicked her every action. The rhythm of the song was now faster and so was her leg movement on the plate. The fireflies swirled around her, switching their light on and off in a rhythmic swirl, sometimes dancing over her head, sometimes moving to her feet, sometimes at her head level.

As the beat increased and played at a faster pace, she took the pot on her head moving the brass plate with her legs in circular movement. The fireflies too circled on her head in resplendent synchrony. At one frantic moment the fireflies in dancing ecstasy whirled inside the pot trying to become one with the dancer's movement. Parasuram quickly put a lid as Sravanya bent lower. The fireflies were trapped inside the pot. Parasuram took the pot from her head and gently laid it down. The song on the tape ended filling the cave with silence.

Sravanya laughed and clapped her hands, "Yaay! We did it."

Bangaru Babu slowly rose from his position and he applauded with a heartful grin. Just then, something coiled around his feet, squeezing them in. The twigs from the shrub grew long to reach Bangaru Babu's feet and were dragging him.

A sudden epiphany hit Parasuram. He yelled, "Bangaru Babu, it is not only the fireflies but also the shrub. We have only weakened Bhushan but did not disable him completely."

Sravanya shrieked. The twigs kept growing and oncoming. She trembled as she saw a twig coiling around Parasuram, reaching faster up to his waist. Sravanya tried to pull the creeper and free Parasuram but her fingers got scraped and blood started to drip from the cuts.

Bangaru Babu threw a knife at Parasuram. He cut the creeper and rushed to Bangaru Babu to free him from the coiled twigs. He tried to cut the twigs to free Bangaru Babu, but it was a futile effort. In panic he screamed, "Bangaram, we have to pluck out the shrub. That is the only way to save ourselves." Parasuram's words hit Bangaru Babu and Sravanya like hot waves urging them into action.

The twigs had not touched Sravanya yet. Bangaru Babu and Parasuram were trying to free themselves from them. She could see that the power of the demon was dwindling. She rushed to the shrub and started to pluck it out using her full power. But her strength did not stand by her. More blood splattered from her hands as they got scraped. The twigs kept on coming, grabbed her by the waist and pushed her far away. The mighty force of the shrub made her twirl many times before she fell on the floor and landed on the pot.

Smaaaash!

The clay pot broke…

The bugs were freed…

All of them froze in cold terror…

The light bugs glowed violently preparing themselves for attack.

The strength of the twigs increased, and they squeezed Parasuram and Bangaru Babu harder, faster.

Bangaru Babu cut all the twigs that were strangling Parasuram by then. He pleaded with Parasuram, "Take *Akka* and get out of the cave. I will distract them."

But before Parasuram could reach Sravanya, a bunch of creepers pulled Sravanya by coiling them to her stomach and pushed her out of the cave. She fell out from the cave's mouth, bruising her hands and legs. Her ribs were wounded by the fall and small stones pierced all over her body. Parasuram went out after her to check if she was alright. But the fireflies stood in his path. Bangaru Babu threw a broken piece of the clay pot at them attracting them towards him.

Bangaru Babu removed the jacket he was wearing and tried to shoo them off. One of the twigs had caught him in his leg and it yanked him down. His knife dropped from his hand. Lying on his back he used his jacket to drive out the bugs, but there were too many for him to handle. One of the creepers coiled itself around his neck and throttled him to death.

He struggled, his hands and legs beating vigorously on the floor, and they gave up after putting up a good fight. His chest that rose to take the breath did not fall. It froze. The heart stopped. His eyes did not blink. They were wide open.

As Parasuram was helping Sravanya to get up and making her sit on a boulder, Bangaru Babu's dead body was thrown out by a bunch of twigs. Sravanya shrieked in horror, her bleeding hands cupped on her face. She let out a painful sob. Parasuram froze in pain. He puked on a stone nearby, yellow bile making an asymmetrical pattern on the stone. He heard a voice, loud and clear. There was no one speaking. But he heard it in his mind.

The message was clear, "Next time I will kill you."

For some time Parasuram was in a trance. He did not know what to do. Should he grieve his son's death? Or should he take Sravanya to the hospital? Bangaru Babu was not his biological son. But they had raised him. Tears streamed down his cheeks. Sravanya was sobbing hysterically, she needed medical attention. She was bleeding. She could die of blood loss. The cave and the surroundings had fallen silent. There was no buzz, no lights. Darkness had set in. If he sat there doing nothing, his daughter would also die. He had to think fast.

He took out the mobile from Bangaru Babu's pocket. His fingers trembled as they touched his body. There was a faint signal. He dialled Sravanya's father's number. He was brief. He asked him to come to the fort and that Sravanya was hurt. From the other side he heard many questions. He did not answer. He asked him to hurry and cut the line. He then helped Sravanya to walk and slowly they climbed down the fort in the moonlight. As they crossed the fort, he looked back and saw the watchers (boulders at the foot of the fort) watching them. He knew they were safe, because if Bhushan had intended to kill them, they both would have been dead by now. They climbed down the steps slowly.

Sravanya was tired. She could not walk further. Parasuram was too old to carry her on her shoulders. He begged her to gather her strength and try her best to walk. If she died there, Bangaru's sacrifice would be in vain. They wanted to honour Bangaru Babu. They trudged down slowly and by the time they reached down, Nanna and Amma had already arrived. Amma ran towards her daughter in shock but relieved to see her alive. Nanna alighted from the car and gave her some water to drink.

"What happened?" he asked.

"Long story," Parasuram replied. "Take her to hospital. Don't tell anyone she was at the fort. Just make something up. Go now."

"But you are wounded too. Come with us," Sravanya's mother said.

"I can't come. I have something to take care of."

After they left, Parasuram made another call to the police inspector. He slowly started to climb up the fort, the watchers watching him, the blood on his hands looked black in the moonlight, his heart broken, his spirit shaken, a dead son, a wounded daughter, and a ghost to kill.

Chapter - 11

To say that Ravi felt awkward about the predicament would be a mere understatement. He was disappointed, angry, and embarrassed. One could not blame him for not confronting his friend and running away, because it was also true that he had gone through an awful trial of sorts. He was mesmerised by Kiranmayi's dance and had a crush on her. He vividly remembered the adrenaline rush that went through his body when he planned to meet her, but the discovery that Kiranmayi was Kiran was not merely being snubbed by fate, it was a huge emotional shock.

Kiran's lack of trust was one thing. The fact that Ravi couldn't decipher from Kiranmayi's photos that she was Kiran was another and it bothered him too much. He should have found out about her long back. One can cheat the world, but a best friend too? Kiran turned out to be a master of make-up and disguise and this fact just made the awkwardness worse.

How shocking and laughable at the same time the whole episode made him feel. It was as if he was reduced to a dark shadow of irreverence in the hands of fate and the whims of a friend. Oh, he tried hard to forget the indignities of his current condition. Ravi tried to remember the days when he and Kiran would just sit around and converse like two normal men, but now it seemed as though thinking such a thing was like dreaming to touch the moon.

His *pinni* (maternal aunt), Sunanda, his mother's younger sister, lived in Hyderabad. Her son, Ramana, who was a year younger to Ravi, was more of a friend than a cousin. Ramana worked in a software company. Ravi and Ramana, had common tastes in movies and IPL. They always had plenty of things to discuss as well and Ravi recalled the times when as teenagers they would often sit on the rooftop and talk endlessly—or until his aunt would call them down for snacks or dinner.

Sunanda *pinni* had been asking him to visit them since the last time he came was almost a year ago. Ravi thought it was the perfect time to meet them. He missed his cousin as well and knew that if he spent some time away from his office, it would do him good. Ravi took a bus to Hyderabad the next morning — without telling Kiran — and reached his *pinni's* house the next morning.

Pinni and *Babai* inquired about his wellbeing and the town as they had heard about the mysterious killings. They were concerned about his safety. Sunanda *pinni* made a scrumptious breakfast for Ravi. She made *puri* and *upma*, but her *vadas* were the best! They tasted just like he had eaten them when he had been to Hyderabad last year.

After breakfast, Ravi and Ramana went to the rooftop to talk like usual. Ramana asked after his office life and how he had been doing all these months.

Although Ravi sounded and looked cheerful, Ramana detected that he wasn't himself and that something was wrong. "Ravi, is something wrong?" He asked directly.

Ravi was vehement. "No, why do you ask?"

"Nothing. Your face tells me something is wrong… You feel distant, bro."

"It's nothing, trust me. I'm good."

Ramana nodded. After a brief silence Ramana said, "You know what? Let's trip across the city on Friday and the weekend. It will cheer you up and though you aren't telling me about it, I do feel that you have an issue."

Ramana thought of Ravi as a friend as well and he wanted to have his friend in his usual cheerful self.

"Okay," Ravi simply nodded. "But don't you have to attend office tomorrow?"

"I will take leave." He smiled at his cousin.

"Not required. I have taken this entire week off. We can roam around the city this weekend. I will rest today. It's just so much of work stress, I don't feel too enthusiastic for a trip." Ravi tried to smile. Ramana nodded and went away for work.

During the weekdays, Ravi napped most of the time as Ramana went to work. He helped his *pinni* and *babai* in running errands and discuss TV shows.

There were a few messages from Kiran but Ravi did not reply. He felt a little emotional seeing Kiran's texts. Ramana took off on Friday and they roamed the city the entire weekend.

Hyderabad's mornings were the best. The greenery, the blue skies, and the bustle of people leaving their homes for work in the morning was something Ravi wished he could find in his town. The duo drove to Gachibowli on Ramana's Honda Activa, scooted around the IKEA mall, went to Inorbit Mall, and then went to a friend of Ramana's who lived in an apartment that was on the 100-feet road of Madhapur. The three of them conversed all afternoon to their heart's content. They talked about Hitech city girls, new movie releases, watched comedy trailers and stand-alone on Netflix and even drank a beer or two.

Ravi started enjoying the trip very much. He was positively distracted and didn't think about Kiran at all.

"I would like to visit you again, bro," Ravi told Ramana's friend and they fist-bumped each other.

They left the friend's house and decided to watch a movie. The nearest theatre was the PVR ICON multiplex adjacent to the HITEC City Metro Rail Station. They booked tickets for an English movie. It was an action-packed one that they thoroughly enjoyed. After the movie, they went to the food court and ordered sandwiches, frankies, and soft drinks.

At an adjacent table were a man and a woman discussing novels and literature. Dressed in a sleeveless, light grey top the charming lady was ebullient and brimming with ideas. Once in a while the man would say something funny and the woman would laugh out loud, "You're too much." The man was in a full sleeved business casual shirt and was thoughtfully replying to the woman's suggestions, agreeing to most of what she was saying. In one particular novel they were writing, she said, we need to add connectors to the beats of our story. The man nodded.

Ravi had heard of cultural spaces like Lamakaan where one sees artists and writers working on their projects but creativity in a mall? Now, that was a pleasant surprise to him.

After filling themselves, Ravi and Ramana returned home. Ravi thanked Ramana for taking him out. They said goodnight to each other and went to their rooms.

Ravi slept peacefully that night and even though he saw images of Kiran in his mind's eyes, his tiredness got the best of him and he fell into a deep slumber.

Next morning came and it was another young men's day out. Ravi and Ramana went to the Galleria Mall. They played bowling, ate at Chutney's and roamed a little in Ameerpet.

Late evening, after they reached home, Ravi partook *pinni's* dinner. "You must come again, okay, Ravi?" Sunanda said.

"Of course," Ravi smiled and nodded. "I would surely miss your *vadas* and this amazing lemon rice though."

She smiled and served another spoonful of lemon rice to Ravi. "Please stop *pinni*. I'm already full!"

"You should eat well since you're traveling. I will also pack some for you in a box. It's not healthy to eat anywhere outside, okay?"

"Okay… okay… *pinni*," Ravi said with a broad smile. Sunanda put the dish bowl down and went to the kitchen to bring a tiffin box for Ravi.

Earlier in the day, Ravi had booked a bus ticket through an app and luckily there were a lot of buses available. Ravi bid farewell to his uncle and aunt. Ramana dropped Ravi on his scooter at the bus pick-up point.

Ravi thanked Ramana, "Thanks *raa*, I had a lot of fun."

"Stop saying thanks, Ravi. The days passed off real quick."

"Yeah."

"So when do you plan on coming back?"

"Soon," Ravi chuckled and lightly punched Ramana's shoulder, "Take care of *pinni* and *babai* and stay in touch."

Ramana nodded.

The night ride on the bus was uneventful. Ravi read some magazines while listening to some music. He was trying to get some sleep, but he couldn't. So, he ended up looking outside at the dark woods that passed by.

The Hyderabad visit made him feel much better. The vastness of the city provided for some level of anonymity, he realised. His town, like every town and village had its idiosyncrasies, its own norms, and its own code of morality. He started empathizing with Kiran. He probably had his reasons.

Killing time in the city would never be an issue. Suddenly he remembered the killings in his town, those weren't resolved yet. Maybe just like in Hyderabad, they too should have CCTV cameras everywhere. He read in the newspaper that the police there were increasingly relying and benefiting from the large number of CCTV cameras.

He remembered Parasuram. Mamayya had taken Ravi's help many times in the past to prepare representations for the government. He even made the required annexures and affidavits. Those were the first drafts, and they were vetted by lawyers for the accuracy of legal information. They seldom caught any problem and were impressed by Ravi's grammar and vocabulary. Mamayya, in particular, liked to get important documentation work prepared by Ravi as he was quite adept in both English and Telugu.

Yes. He should definitely meet Mamayya as early as possible and talk to him about the matter.

*****

SI and the police team arrived sometime around midnight. Parasuram's head was buried in his hands. Suresh Pidugu tapped on his shoulder lightly. Parasuram looked at him, his eyes red, his face pinched, weary and wrinkled. He looked old, very old.

"What happened?" Inspector Suresh asked him.

Parasuram couldn't speak anything for a brief moment. He looked dazed. "We came here... and... um... we found Bangaru Babu dead." He broke into a sob. He stammered the last sentence, "That cave is a monster." He cried again.

"It is too dark to check that cave. We will come tomorrow morning," SI replied.

"You want to change your story?" SI's question broke his thought process.

"What do you mean?"

"I am arresting you for the murder of Bangaru Babu."

"I did not. What I told you is true. I did not cook up some story." His mind was dazed by the grief that he started to weep again.

The SI did not say anything. He handcuffed Parasuram and took him into police custody. There was an ambulance shortly which took Bangaru Babu's body to the police station. The paramedics from the ambulance cleaned and applied antiseptic cream on his wounds. Parasuram had to spend that night in jail. Next morning, Sravanya's father came to meet Parasuram but the SI would not allow him to meet. "Sir, I just want to meet him for two minutes. That's all." He requested.

"And what is so urgent that you want to meet a murderer and can't wait. I am building a case here. I don't have time." He shouted at Niladri Mullapudi.

"Parasuram could not have killed Bangaru Babu. If he really wanted to kill him, he could have killed him at so many other places. He had a lot of opportunities. Why take him to that fort and murder him? And what could be the motive?"

The inspector gave a serious thought to his suggestion. "There was no one there. And he kept on talking about the cave." The inspector was lost in his thoughts.

"Sir, if you can please allow me for two minutes. I will not take much time." Niladri asked again.

The inspector nodded and accompanied him to Parasuram's cell. Parasuram came up to the cell's bars seeing Niladri who signalled him that everything was alright with his nod. Parasuram held his hands and thanked him. SI Suresh did not understand a thing. He thought there was something more to what Parasuram put up.

After Niladri left, he took two constables to the fort to examine the cave. He wanted to take another look. It was a bright day and the sun glared at them in all its radiance. They wiped their sweat and took more time than usual to hike up the hill. SI Suresh was not physically fit and his large paunch was definitely not a good indicator of his fitness. He panted and took short breaks. Even the constables were irritated by him. They wanted to finish the hike so that they don't have to face the sun, but SI Suresh kept on halting.

Finally, they reached the top and went into the cave. Inside everything was pitch black. There were flashlights, a broken mud pot, there was a camera, but it was broken. No use of switching it on as whatever was recorded must have been gone. They collected all of the scattered things and tagged them in evidence bags. They brought emergency lights with them which brightened up the cave even to the farthest corners where the sunlight from the opening did not reach.

There was no sight of creepers or twigs that Parasuram had earlier talked about. There was only one dead shrub in a faraway corner in the dark. Other than that, there was nothing in the cave. There was splattered and dried blood on the floor. Bangaru Babu was murdered here. And Parasuram might have carried the body outside. They must have argued over something which might have enraged Parasuram and then must have killed them. What was it were they arguing about? Could it be that Parasuram was the serial murderer, Bangaru Babu found that out and when confronted, Parasuram killed Bangaru Babu? Perfect! That way he could pin all the murders on Parasuram. He had to build the story more and have the evidence manipulated in such a way that all of that pointed to Parasuram.

On his way back he decided to call Subramanyam and other journalists to give an elaborate interview. He would just leave the hints in the air. The journalists will do their job in building the details. And Seshadri would add more fuel to his story. He smiled and dozed off in the police jeep back to the station tired from the hike.

In the meantime, word spread out that Bangaru Babu was killed and Parasuram was wounded and arrested as a suspect for the murder of Bangaru Babu. News channels as usual added more fuel to the fire. There were news scripts running, existing broadcasts were cancelled and Parasuram's arrest became the highlight of the morning news.

As soon as the inspector reached the station, a little over 2 pm driver Raju was waiting for him. "Sir, Parasuram Mamayya was with me last night when Bangaru Babu was murdered." Driver Raju spoke abruptly.

SI Suresh sat on his chair, put a *paan* inside his mouth, "What? Are you in your senses? Why were you not there then at the scene of the murder? Or are you also the co-conspirator?"

"No Sir. I can prove it. This is a recording of Bangaru Babu's call to me yesterday evening before he went up that hill." He played the recording. "Raju, I am going to the fort and to the cave. I will kill the ghost. Please trust your friend and come back."

"A ghost?" Inspector's eyes widened. The two constables who went up the fort with the SI looked at each other's faces.

"Bangaru Babu believed there was a ghost in that cave that killed the people. I got worried when I heard this recording and rushed back to Parasuram Mamayya's house. He was equally shocked." Bangaru Babu swallowed, took a breath, and continued, "We went up the fort. There was no sign of Bangaru Babu and so we went into the wild and then to the cave. We found Bangaru Babu's dead body and called you. Mamayya was grief stricken and went into a frenzy state. Because of the shock he started laughing and crying, he was behaving like a mad man. Since the signal was low, I hiked down to get some help. I met with an accident. I drove my auto straight into a tree just a few miles away from the fort on the road and fell unconscious. Today morning I woke up and immediately came to the station to tell you the whole thing. Sir, if you don't believe me, you can check my auto which I dashed into a tree in panic. And see sir, I have wounds as well, on my face and arms." He showed his wounds.

"Are you telling the truth? If you are telling any lies, we will know. If not now, subsequently." SI glared at him as if he would kill him. This guy complicated the case.

Niladri Mullapudi walked in with a lawyer who had the anticipatory bail ready. It was all planned. The judge had granted interim bail. The SI had to make a stronger case against Parasuram because he had a witness now. It could be that Raju was blatantly lying but for now Parasuram would be released on bail. Suresh sighed.

Parasuram was released. There was a crowd of journalists, TV anchors and photographers outside the police stations waiting to ask him a bunch of questions. They all rushed to him seeing him coming out and bombarded him with an array of questions. Driver Raju shielded him from the cameras and the photographers and with great difficulty led him to their car.

He took Parasuram home and gave him a glass of water. Parasuram's mobile beeped continuously. It was his wife Malati. He will talk to her in a while. But first he must thank Raju who sat down and was crying like a small child, grieving his friend's death.

"I should not have fled. I should have come with you people. It is because of me that my friend is dead. I want to help. I will not flee again. Together we will stop it." Driver Raju broke into a series of sobs.

*****

Ravi woke up before the bus reached his town. It pulled into the station and Ravi got down. The soft breeze, the smell of the coals and fresh flowers which the vendors were selling lingered in the air. He headed towards the exit, slinging his backpack on his shoulder and to his surprise noticed Parasuram walking towards the exit as well. Quite a coincidence!

Mamayya…what's he doing here? Ravi thought and hastened towards Parasuram so that he could ask for an appropriate time for them to meet up. He stopped in front of him breathing heavily but smiling as well.

"*Namasakram* Mamayya!" Ravi greeted.

"O, Ravi, you surprised me! How are you? Where had you gone?" Parasuram asked, noticing Ravi's bag on his shoulder.

"I'm fine, Mamayya. I went to Hyderabad last week to visit Sunanda *pinni* and Raghava *babai*."

"All well with them?"

"Yes, Mamayya," Ravi and Parasuram began walking past the coolies and the small stalls that sold water bottles, paan, cigarettes, and snacks. They exited the station. "How come you are here?"

"I had come to see off an old friend of mine from another village."

Ravi observed that Parasuram was limping to his right, "What is this Mamayya?" He asked with a frown, "You're limping slightly, and your left shoulder seems to be swollen."

"Ravi, haven't you seen yesterday's news?" Ravi shook his head. Parasuram smiled. "I will tell you some other time."

"Mamayya, I wanted to meet you and talk to you about getting CCTV cameras installed all around the town and the fort to nab the killer. We can prepare a presentation to the government and submit it quickly. Since this is an emergency situation, funds will be sanctioned immediately. When shall I come and meet you to prepare the drafts?"

Parasuram stopped and so did Ravi.

"CCTV cameras won't help!" Parasuram said in a firm tone.

Ravi was puzzled upon his sudden reaction, "Why not, Mamayya? But in Hyderabad…"

Parasuram cut Ravi off, "Let us go to a restaurant and talk. You need to know something important and you need to keep it confidential."

"Sure, Mamayya."

Ravi and Parasuram headed to the nearest restaurant in silence.

*****

Parasuram and Ravi found a table in a corner that was silent. Not even the sound of the auto-rickshaws or the mumblings of the people could be heard. Parasuram ordered coffee for both of them. Parasuram recounted the brief history of Bhushan who did not harm female dancers and narrated the failed attempt with Sravanya.

"Sravanya, Bangaru Babu, and I approached the fort. There we saw the fireflies and followed it to their source which was deep inside the fort," Parasuram's face was serious as he spoke with a heavy voice, "Sravanya was performing a difficult dance in front of Bhushan and something wonderful happened." His eyes grew slightly wide, "As she started dancing, the fireflies twirled and swayed around her."

Ravi's mouth opened a little as he listened to Parasuram in silence. Parasuram could see the flashbacks play in front of his eyes as though he was watching a film reel. He was reliving the events that happened that night and he could feel something — like a gravitational pull — tug at his stomach. His tone betrayed his desperation. But he stayed strong and continued. "Sravanya used an earthen pot in her dance and one point of time, the fireflies just entered the pot, and I closed the lid, thinking that she caught the ghost. But then, Bhushan — the ghost, got angry…"

Parasuram gulped slowly, "There was a shrub that attacked Sravanya and dragged her with one of its extended creepers. Sravanya took a fall and the earthen pot broke. The fireflies escaped while Sravanya tried to fight with the shrub but her strength wasn't enough. She fell back, losing the grip from the twig and rolled down farther from the shrub..." Parasuram sighed and rubbed his forehead. His eyes were glazed, and Ravi dared not interrupt him.

"I ran towards her, but the fireflies swarmed around me. I eventually pulled her and we rushed outside. But Bangaru Babu was killed by the shrub. He saved both our lives and wasn't able to save his life. I was arrested by the police as a suspect. But driver Raju gave a false alibi, and I was released on anticipatory bail." He fell silent.

Ravi was a person who could be trusted. And so he narrated the whole incident to him without hiding any of the facts he knew. And now that Bangaru Babu was gone, he needed another soldier in his team, someone strong, witty and quick in thinking. Ravi fit the description. He was a good replacement to Bangaru Babu. Now they were left with finding a dancer. Sravanya's strength was not enough to pull the shrub or even to pull herself away from the clutches of the shrub.

Ravi was in utter disbelief and pondered again and again over the repressive supernatural transgression conveyed to him. Mamayya was the one to who people came seeking for help and he now was sitting in front of Ravi in a mood of desperation. No, it was not Mamayya alone; it was the whole village that seemed to stand before him vulnerable. Why was life playing these tricks? Ravi wanted to cry out loud. A ghost, of all things? The sullen mood of an untrusting friend that he so well overcame by going out of town, the normalcy he recreated in his heart, was all but gone now. Did life forbid repose?

Parasuram drank his coffee but Ravi's turned cold. He sipped it once but grimaced as the cold coffee touched his lips. He put it down and pushed the cup aside. Parasuram knew that it would take a while for the youngster to digest the situation. He remained silent.

A few minutes passed in silence and then Ravi shook his head as if coming out of a stupor. He found his bearings and then shot a barrage of questions like an inquisitive child, also implicitly offering solutions.

"Why don't you try *tantriks*, Mamayya? They will surely get rid of the ghost in no time."

Parasuram sighed and shook his head, "We did. But he was killed too. Ruthlessly."

"Why don't you bring witches or black magic practitioners?" Ravi shot next.

"Bhushan won't fall under their spell. He surrendered himself to God before he was killed. The surrender built into an internal energy core that is protecting him."

Ravi couldn't stop himself. "Why don't you call the police? Or get guns and cannons and blast the fort?" His adrenaline had kicked hard, and it was hard for Ravi to stop his leg from shaking as well underneath the table.

"Bhushan may still find another refuge. Also, remember, we want to retain the fort and develop it. So that's a no go."

"Okay, so if you're not blasting the fort, can you try limited area digging with earth movers and quarry mining?"

Parasuram's eyebrows rose high along with his eyes. It became apparent to Ravi that he was feeling slightly annoyed by Ravi's suggestive questions.

"What, young man? Getting quarry miners here is illegal."

Ravi held back another question that was stirring in his mind, "Sorry, Mamayya… I just got a bit emotional and blabbered away."

Parasuram's expressions softened as he leaned back on his chair and sighed, "I understand the noble intentions behind your angst. The only way that will work is the way I tried."

"Once again, sorry, Mamayya. I can't get a female South Indian classical dancer for you."

"Well, if you are ready to help…" Parasuram was silent for a moment or two before he took in a deep breath, "This time, I want someone different."

Ravi felt a surge of respect for the senior man, he was Nachiketa, one who does not let his energy be lost, never to give up, ghost or not.

He leaned forward. "Whom do you want, Mamayya?"

Parasuram adjusted himself in his seat, "The only thing that we lacked in Sravanya was the bodily strength of a well-built man. I want a male dancer who dresses and dances like a woman. If we can't get such a person here, you try to find one in Hyderabad. In fact, the visitor whom I came to drop by was an old friend, a retired dance guru. I asked him to find me a male dancer who is ready to risk his life for the community good."

Ravi's eyes grew wide at once.

"Or we will train a young man with a crash course in classical South Indian dance," Parasuram continued.

Ravi's face glowed like a neon lamp in darkness. He wasn't sure if he was being selfish or if he was accepting of the fact that Kiran was who he was and no one could change him now, but he knew that Kiran was the perfect answer to this uncanny problem.

"No need to go anywhere or train anybody, Mamayya," Ravi said with a hint of glee in his tone, "We will get Kiran."

Parasuram frowned and stared at Ravi questioningly, "I don't get it. Kiran? Your friend? But how?"

"Yes, Mamayya, you heard it right," Ravi couldn't stop smiling. "Your requirements are met, for Kiranmayi is Kiran."

*****

The next day, Kiran and Ravi ignored each other. Kiran attempted to spark a conversation with Ravi but Ravi deftly avoided him. He would either act as though he got a call or just walk past Kiran and go to another colleague from their department. Kiran was annoyed but he tried his best to stay calm and hoped to try talking to Ravi the next day.

However, Ravi yet again turned a blind eye to Kiran as if he was just a crumpled paper near the dustbin. While Kiran sat in his chair and wondered how he would be able to talk to Ravi, the office blacked out. Everyone began to stand up and look around at each other. Ravi and Kiran glanced at each other but neither of them reacted like the others. They quickly looked away and asked the others what had happened.

Peon Ramalingam came rushing and told everyone to stay calm. "We don't know when electricity will be restored. But there is a problem even with the backup diesel generator. We will try to get it fixed as soon as possible but it could take about one and a half hours."

Most of the staff were annoyed since they needed the internet to work, while others were happy that they got a bit of a break. Everyone began to light up candles or turn on their flashlights.

Kiran pursed his lips and took this opportunity to walk over to Ravi's desk to break the ice.

"Hey Ravi," Kiran spoke with a soft smile. "Instead of sitting in the dark, let's go to Chinna's and eat something."

"I'm not hungry."

Chinna was the fellow who ran a mobile cart snack centre just around the block. It was a short walk from their office and he was Kiran's and Ravi's favourite street vendor. One thing they savoured most was the *Mirapakaya Bajjilu*. Those were out of the world and he thought taking Ravi there would do the trick.

"I'm not interested," Ravi cut Kiran sharply.

Kaushalya was looking intently at them knitting a sweater. "You two fought?" She asked. They both shook their heads. "If you are going out, please get a plate for me, too."

Sarma Sir jumped in, "For me too, a plate of every item he has."

Kiran smiled giving an approving nod to them.

"Oh, come on!" Kiran insisted. "You can hardly do any work without electricity and with the sun beginning to set, there's hardly any light here. What will you do staying here in the dark? And for how long will you not talk to me?" He crossed his arms. "I said I will clear the air. So, please, just hear me out."

Ravi bit the insides of his cheeks but there was still a glare in his eyes as he stared at Kiran. Ravi could only see a fraction of Kiran's face because of someone else's flashlight that illuminated part of the office.

Ravi slowly nodded and stood up. Kiran smiled a little, turned around and walked towards the exit. Ravi followed suit to Chinna's stall.

"You see, by the time they come back, they will be laughing and cracking jokes and will be like old selves again." Sarma Sir told Kaushalya who smiled without looking at him busy knitting a sweater.

Chinna's stall wasn't crowded which was a good thing for the both of them. There were just two customers, men who had just finished eating and were drinking tea. Chinna welcomed Ravi and Kiran with a huge smile.

"How are you, Chinna?" Kiran asked.

"Good, good, how are you, Kiran sir?" Chinna smiled.

"I'm doing fine," Kiran smiled back and looked for a few seconds through the glass walls of the mobile cart. His mouth was already salivating as he stared at the crispy and delicious looking snacks.

He ordered their favourites -- two plates each with *punugulu*, two *mirapakaya bajjilu*, two *aaloo bonda*s and one egg *bajji*. Chinna served them with a profuse addition of coconut chutney and ginger chutney.

Kiran paid the money, took the plates and gave one to Ravi. Both of them stepped away from the cart and stood under the tall tree that had a single lightbulb somewhere between the leaves hanging from it.

Ravi ate in silence but Kiran brought him here to talk, so after eating a *mirapakaya bajji* -- the spice tingled in his mouth and the hotness of the *bajji* made it worse -- he broke the silence that had enveloped them.

"Ravi...I had to conceal my identity because of societal pressures."

"A cop out, I knew you would say that. An evolved individual, a fighter you are not," Ravi said.

"I don't want to comment on that statement," Kiran said, trying his best to stay collected. "Seriously, I didn't want to take additional burden over and above practicing my dance skills and establishing myself so that Kiranmayi is a successful dancer. Yes, there are societal pressures, and you know that as much as I do."

"Okay, since you're repeating the term, what kind of societal pressures are you talking about?"

Kiran sighed heavily to reduce the spiciness of the *mirapakaya bajji* piece he had just eaten. He made an O with his mouth and blew out a long draw of air.

"First of all, people are disrespectful of dancers. There are some crazy perverts who think all dancers have loose character and are ersatz prostitutes."

"Whoa!" Ravi's eyes grew wide. "But the South Indian classical dancing is considered sacred. How can people have such views?"

"Not *all*. I said there were *some* crazy perverts."

Ravi pursed his lips thoughtfully. He dipped a *punugu* in the chutney and took a bite. "Well, if that's the case, if you revealed Kiranmayi is you, the problem would just disappear."

Kiran took a bite of his egg *bajji* and licked his fingers that had the chutney on it.

"That will bring in a lot of other problems."

"Like?"

"A whole plethora! First people would dig up my caste and keep shouting around my Backward Classes caste. 'How can a backward caste guy do sacred dances?'"

"Did that actually happen to any?"

"More than you think. Some narrow-minded people from the upward castes would cause this kind of problem from behind the scenes."

"Hmm… I guess so. Caste has not yet disappeared from society. Many decision makers give more importance to it than merit."

"Not only there would be opposition based on my caste, but also everything I do in my dance will be under microscopic scrutiny."

"Come again, how will that be a problem?"

Kiran let out a soft sigh. "If I try a slight variation or improvement, even a subtle or faintest one in a movement, gesture, or posture, the critics would fall on me like a ton of bricks. 'This guy committed a hara-kiri, a sacrilege', 'Does he even know the basics of dance?', 'Is he fit to carry on the *divine* tradition of dance?', and on and on, but you get the idea."

Ravi nodded, "Got it."

"And the information would be known in our office. I would have to face crude jokes daily."

"I wouldn't have done that nor would I ever do that—to you or anyone else."

"I know! But some jerks would say, 'Is this guy really a man or a transgender?' as if that's funny. Others might ask, 'When you are dressed as a female for dance, do men hit on you? Do they chase you for sex?'"

Kiran had a deep frown on his face. Ravi could see how much he was hurting and how much he had to think just to do something that he loved.

"You know what these so-called jokes reflect?" Kiran asked but Ravi just stayed silent. "That there is no understanding or empathy not just for the transgenders but also for the entire LGBTQ community in India. That's what it really means."

The conversation ended there. Both of them finished their snacks, crumpled up the paper plates and threw them into the dustbin. There was a plastic mineral water can with a tap on a stool and a broken bucket right underneath it. It was a drinking water and a wash basin area!

Kiran took a plastic glass from above the mineral water can, rinsed the glass and threw the water in the bucket. He then filled the glass with water and drank from it. After he was done, he handed the glass to Ravi who filled it too and drank from it.

With their tummies full and their mouth still tingling from the *mirpakaya bajji*, they went back to the office with plates of snacks for their colleagues.

Kiran and Ravi stopped near the entrance.

"I hope you now understand that I blew away a lot of potential problems coming on to me by creating an identity called Kiranmayi," Kiran said with a small smile.

"Yes, I hear you," Ravi said. "But what I don't understand is that you didn't value our friendship enough to trust me."

Chapter - 12

Varada Reddy sat in his tiny little office and called Sravanya just to re-check that she was getting ready for her performance. However, Sravanya didn't answer the call.

Varada was well-known for organizing memorable events. He was a good-hearted soul and always arranged decent monetary compensation to artists who performed at his events. Even if the events were free for the audience, he never for once disregarded any performer and compensated them for their hard work.

He had a knack for finding sponsors. If he couldn't get any funds, he would at least pay them from his own pocket. The artists would often be surprised by Varada's large heartedness and would always await his call.

He used to always wonder when the town's temple would call him and ask for his help. This year was the turning point. The temple committee had authorised Varada to conduct the *Dasara* festival events. He was excited and couldn't believe his ears when they asked him to take care of all the events for the entire duration of the festival.

Apparently, the gods had heard his prayer and granted him this opportunity to showcase his talent to the worshippers, priests, and visitors alike. For the main dance event, he had booked the best dancer in the town, Sravanya.

*****

Varada waited for fifteen minutes before he dialled her number again. This time Sravanya picked up the call but her voice was feeble and slow. There was a hint of exhaustion in it.

"Hello?"

"Madam," Varada uttered with a sigh of relief. "Just a normal call, hope you are all set for the dance programme and there are no hitches."

"Reddy *garu*, it's good that you called. I wanted to message you, but I couldn't...the thing is, I can't make it."

Varada Reddy's eyes grew wide and his body froze for a couple of moments. "Oh no! Why?"

"It's a long story. I will tell you later," she said and breathed out heavily. "I am badly injured and am in the hospital now."

Varada was shocked and was on the edge of the seat. "Madam! What happened? Are you alright?" He was worried about Sravanya more than the event.

"The doctors are still taking medical tests," she replied. "I have cuts and bruises. As of now, I understand that there are no bone fractures."

"That's some relief," he sighed and leaned back on his chair. "Take care Sravanya *garu*. Please let me know if there is anything that I can help you with."

"Of course, take care, bye." Sravanya disconnected the call.

Varada Reddy was in a state of turmoil. Now who would dance at the *Dasara* event? He wondered who was on par with Sravanya. Who else but Kiranmayi!

He immediately called Kiranmayi's manager's number and waited for him to pick up. Varada Reddy didn't know the manager's full name. He was known by a simple and unforgettable name, Rao.

After a few rings, he heard a click from the other side. So he said, "Hello, is this Rao *garu*?"

A deep-set voice spoke from the other end. "Yes."

"Hello, Rao *garu*. This is Varada Reddy. How are you?"

"I'm good and how are you?"

"To be honest, I am in a small crisis. I am organizing the cultural events for the *Dasara* celebrations, but the dance artist cancelled…"

"Oh, right, I heard it was Sravanya, right?"

"Yes, it is."

Varada Reddy stood up from his seat and paced around the room anxiously.

"What happened to her?" Rao asked.

"She said she was injured and hospitalised. I don't know how she got injured though."

"Injured?" There was evident surprise in Rao's voice.

"She will recover soon I think based on what she told me."

"That's good. However, Kiranmayi is not available on those days. She got a lot of requests, but she is going on a vacation."

"Could you please put in a strong request?" Varada Reddy rubbed his forehead. "The dance programme has already been announced."

"Not possible Reddy *garu*. Madam is not available on those dates."

Varada Reddy sighed and slumped his shoulders. "Alright, I will try to arrange someone else but if there's any chance that Kiranmayi madam is available, please block her date for our event."

"Okay…"

Varada Reddy hung up the call and walked over to his cabinet and pulled out a logbook where the names, addresses and numbers of other dancers were registered. Varada just hoped he could find a dancer who is as amazing as Sravanya and Kiranmayi on time.

On the other side of the call, Kiran put his phone by his side. Just before Varada Reddy's call, he had taken a shower, put on his *banian* and *lungi* and laid down on the bed. The triple life he lived; that of himself, of Kiranmayi and of Rao -- Kiranmayi's personal manager -- was overwhelming.

And although it was a difficult stride, it was a fascinating, and he dare say, an amusing experience. Of course, the roles he played in his dances were far more bewitching and demanding.

Kiran placed a hand on his forehead and closed his eyes. *Should I have accepted Varada Reddy's request?* He would never say 'no' to dance as he believed it was divine. He, as Kiranmayi, did not have any dance bookings that day and doing it would have been beneficial. In fact, Varada would have been grateful for the rest of his life that Kiranmayi had helped him out in a tough situation. Plus, given Varada's big heart, he would have easily received extra payment from him.

But then as a replacement to Sravanya? No way! I'm done playing the second fiddle. I have moved on.

Kiran stared at the ceiling as he gradually drifted to the past, to the fragments of life in which Kiranmayi was born.

*****

Kiran's feet danced even when he was a toddler. He used to take part in inter-school competitions or in the community festival celebrations. Moreover, his parents supported and cheered him since Kiran danced exceptionally well in different forms, be it filmy or classic.

But then, life is not simple and straightforward.

125

There was this girl who always stole the limelight and got the prizes and accolades. Sravanya. Even when the dance categories were separate and he won the first prize in the boys' category, she would win the first prize among the girls and then everyone would go gaga over her talent and spectacular performance. As if his performance and prize did not matter.

She was the talk of the town and every house would force or urge their daughters to become someone like Sravanya. Kiran couldn't help but feel annoyed that everyone, even his parents, discussed Sravanya at breakfast, lunch and dinner. It made him feel as though he wasn't good enough and led to a quiet determination that he had to beat Sravanya if he wanted the spotlight to shine on only him.

Life is also frequent with turning points.

It so happened that in one of the events, he dressed up as a girl and danced. Kiran had looked at himself in the mirror and felt more like himself than ever. He felt butterflies in his stomach as his name was called but a strange sense of confidence had built up inside him as though this was the moment he had been waiting for all this time.

Kiran remembered being embarrassed and shy after his dance as he stared at the crowd in front of him but to his utter surprise and dismay, the audience went frenzy with thunderous applause. The results were announced. He won the first prize. The event anchor was fulsome with praise and the organisers gave him special gifts as well.

Life is also very confusing at times.

He was sure that this was not the best of his displays and yet... *Why this much appreciation? Was it because the audience prefers girls over boys in dance? Or was it because a boy danced like a girl in a female role, which was an extra effort? Perhaps it had something to do with the looks of the cute Sravanya that fetched her those accolades more than him? Was dance the prerogative of only girls?*

Kiran's mind boggled with these questions and he wished he could point out which was true but he couldn't. At that age, he could only as far comprehend that girls were somehow more important than boys in the society with regards to dancing, singing and arts whereas boys must do all the physical and strenuous work.

He was disappointed on the day that he became the most popular up until that time in his life. The boyhood happiness of winning had vanished quickly and for the time being he just wanted to hide under a rock and never come out. He was confused and had so many questions but there was no one who could answer it for him. Kiran felt lost but dance had found him and guided him into doing something that could take his mind off Sravanya and the missing echoes that played in the back of his mind of the cheering crowd.

Soon after, Kiran slowly began to give regular dance performances as a girl. He wanted to avoid dancing in events that Sravanya was a part of. He somehow managed to gather information about her discreetly, which was tough but worth it since he was trying to avoid Sravanya at all costs.

Over a period of time, he found out a lot about her. They grew up as teenagers and while the informer would ask if he was asking about Sravanya due to a certain infatuation, Kiran was sure that it was just mere distaste. It was strange how he felt that way even though they hadn't really talked to each other. Nevertheless, he kept a tab on her dance events and would refuse to participate in them no matter how much the sponsors requested.

Sravanya, on the other hand, hardly knew about Kiran.

*****

As Kiran drifted off to sleep, at that moment, unbeknownst to him, another man was killed just like the previous victims.

The man was driven into the fort by the fireflies. His neck, waist and leg were strangled by prickly bushes. The thorns pinched his skin, oozing out blood from all over his body. His face was half-burnt, the charred skin and flesh emitting a pungent odour. Blood streamed down from the mouth and across his neck, his eyes were wide open and the sclera of his eyes was red. Blood dripped from the corners of his eyes as well along with hidden tears.

His stomach was indented from inside and out. There were holes visible; the hallmark of the fireflies that had entered through the mouth and erupted out of the belly with bloodstained wings and body. He lay in his own pool of blood, a poor soul who had no idea that he would die such a death.

His skin was burnt, and his intestines were spangled in twisted knots. It was indeed a grotesque dance of death, a macabre feast of revenge.

Chapter - 13

The beating of the sun overhead brought sweat to Parasuram's forehead. The ageing scooter spat and groaned under the stress of two people and the speed they were forcing it to go. There were no alternatives though. A time sensitive mission required that they pushed as hard as they could.

The streets were packed and the little scooter weaved through traffic like a needle in the hands of a well-trained seamstress. Horns beeped, drivers shouted, somewhere in the distance a child cried for its mama, and roadside vendors were calling customers with their products. Every sound and sight was recognised fleetingly only in the back of Parasuram's mind. The front was focused entirely on their destination.

"Wait for me out here, Raju." A curt nod promised that his words had been taken on board, so Parasuram disembarked the scooter and made his way into the building.

Kiran was only an acquaintance. Parasuram could only hope that in the face of imminent danger, he would step up to the challenge and demonstrate to the world his arrival into manhood, courage and heroism. A star could be born. The thought alone brought a humoured smile to his lips.

He rapped his knuckles smartly on the smooth wood of the flat door. Kiran called for him to wait just a minute, and then there were sounds of rustling. The door swung open with relish, and Kiran grinned like a puppy dog, watching the most respected personality of the town at his doorstep, though the widening of his eyes gave away his surprise.

"*Namaste*, Mamayya."

"*Namaste*, Kiran. *Challaga Undu*. May I come in?"

"Uh, sure. Yes. Please come in and have a seat. "

Hope stayed solid in his chest as Parasuram went in.

"May I offer you a glass of water?"

"Please," Parasuram nodded.

So far, so good, Parasuram thought. Kiran was on his best behaviour; that much was certain. The hesitancy in his voice ensured that Parasuram knew he was anxious about what was to come.

Kiran disappeared into the kitchen and returned with a glass of water that had condensation dripping down the sides.

As Parasuram took a sip, Kiran said in a hushful voice, "Mamayya, why did you take the trouble to come to my house? One word on the phone and I'd have landed at your home."

Parasuram took another sip and placed the glass on the side table. Clearing his throat, he said, "There are some things that can't be talked over the phone. This is one such thing."

Kiran nodded respectfully, his face becoming slowly intense as if to convey, 'I am all ears.'

There was no doubt in Parasuram's mind that Kiran, while self-isolated most of the time, was at least aware of the events in the local area. Parasuram's life experiences gave him a keen eye for reactions. Without this, he may not have seen how a slight tension stole up Kiran's back, tightening his shoulders, pushing strings of muscle out on his neck. Hands, dug firmly and insolently in his trousers, began to shake.

"The killings in our town are getting out of control. There is one thing you don't know though. So I have to tell you."

Parasuram described the ghost of a dancer who was born a man but grew the heart of a woman. They were murdered for their ways, which no one at the time understood. The victim of this senseless murder, Bhushan, had returned as a ghost, hell-bent on destroying the town; killing anyone without prejudice.

"Only a talented female dancer can help."

Kiran rolled his eyes and Parasuram could not gauge Kiran's thoughts. He breathed in deeply, refusing to allow his emotions show.

"Then why don't you get a female classical dancer, trick him and destroy him?"

Parasuram corrected him. "Destroying Bhushan is not possible. He has to be mellowed and put in a bottle. Regarding the question of another female dancer, yes, we made the first attempt with Sravanya. Brave girl. She entered the fort. The ghost was mollified. But then she could not overtake him. Her physical strength gave up."

Kiran was flabbergasted. "What, when?" He quickly blurted.

What Parasuram did not realise was that it was Sravanya's name that threw Kiran a little off-balance.

Parasuram replied calmly, "Yes, you heard it right. Lives are at stake here, Kiran. We tried to contain the ghost last week."

"And other's lives matter more than my own? My life won't be at stake? Who do you think you are, asking me of all people to eliminate a transgendered ghost? What part of my life as a *dancer* led you to believe I was equipped to fight, and win against a ghost?"

Parasuram said nothing, knowing that Kiran was not stupid. Childish sometimes, selfish also perhaps, but never stupid. He kept quiet, the faintest of a grin appeared at the corners of his lips.

"You know." Kiran paused in shuddering disbelief. "You want me to fight the ghost. Which means you know about me."

"Yes, Ravi told me. You are Kiranmayi. In the light of recent goings-on, he deemed it necessary."

Muscles jumped up in Kiran's jaw, his frustration rising stark in his otherwise soft, youthful appearance. The news was never expected to be accepted with a smile but Parasuram was now uncertain that he should have admitted who supplied him with that information.

"He had no right. None at all. I can't imagine why... I am not the person you need."

"People are dying."

Self-interest, the primordial human behaviour kicked in. "I know that!" Kiran bellowed, then followed it with a soft, "Obviously, I know that. But what do you believe will come of me telling the world I am Kiranmayi? I've barely earned a reputation as a dancer. Now you want me to reveal that I am Kiranmayi? That I have come to dance as her? For all practical purposes, my dancing career will be over and Kiranmayi would have to be given a silent burial."

Parasuram replied calmly, "We need not tell the world Kiranmayi is you. You just come to the fort dressed as Kiranmayi and start your dance."

Kiran now felt Parasuram was manipulating him.

Kiran shook his head; obviously he was in no mood to listen.

People will know the truth that he is Kiranmayi.

"Your problems are at the personal level, they can be solved. The ghost problem is affecting the whole community. Personal problems can be solved only if we survive." The man with infinite patience, a man of practical wisdom was not going to give up so soon. He continued, "Your problems are that your look at the priorities wrong. You think personal problems sit higher than those of the town. Whatever was troubling you now can be solved after we have dealt with what was troubling the community."

Had Parasuram not been looking, he might not have noticed the half-expression that crossed Kiran's face. Something between hurt and doubled-down certainty.

"Mamayya," Kiran began, his voice even despite the shaking of his hands, "You don't know me as well as you like to think you do. You have no idea what I have been through. You don't know the experiences I had to go through. It is very easy to say personal problems are small and can be solved. I think it's the opposite. A few of you can come together and get rid of the ghost. But the darkness in the hearts of people, it will linger and who will get rid of it?"

The sunlight outside grew brighter. A murder of crows flew past the window, their cawing grated on Parasuram's nerves.

"Kiran, you are not even half of my age. I have seen decades come and go by. How far we have come forward as a society! In dance itself, what was once mundane, became profane, what was profane became scared."

"Sacred and sexist," Kiran hit back immediately.

"Attitudes can be changed. But if it is your identity that is bothering you the most, then we tell no one that you are Kiranmayi, if that is what it takes. You will wear the uniform, dance and subdue the ghost."

"It doesn't matter what you say. People will know."

A mild fury spread from Parasuram's heart to his cheeks, and he repressed the urge to show it. The possibility of saving lives hung on one person.

"Listen Mamayya, I am not interested in the history of dance, and I am losing my patience with your insistence. Here's your solution that you crave so desperately; go to some *tantrik* or *pujari*, ask them for the rituals, and boom! The ghost is gone."

These thoughts had, of course, crossed Parasuram's mind. They had, actually, been among the first to come to him when he became aware of the haunting that plagued his community. However, *tantriks* and *pujaris* would not be enough. Bhushan's ghost was embedded further than what some men of scripture and magic could solve. A special kind of person needed to be employed to eliminate a spirit like this. Kiran was born for this.

Parasuram said, "You have to trust me. Bhushan is not a regular ghost. *Tantriks* and *pujaris* cannot do this. Only a female dancer, one with a strong spiritual connection to dance, can help. As I said, except for female dancers he will be ruthless against everyone else."

"The moment he realises, if he does so, that I am a man, he will eat me alive. The very thought scares me. I worry about my life; the risk of this project gone wrong is my death. Forgive me for caring more about my life than you do."

The words hurt Parasuram in a way that he was not ready to feel. Now was not the time for emotions to interfere, however. He had a mission, and Kiran's contributions were non-negotiable.

"I am looking at this as a sense of duty, as you should be. This duty was to fight the ghost, save the lives of the community and allow their right to safety to come back. I need you to enact these plans. You will come out of this alive, I promise you. Please, trust me."

"All this sounds bizarre. I learnt dance to be a dancer. Not to handle murderous ghosts or to fight. If you can't trust the *tantriks* and priests do their jobs, then rely on the police or army. These people are trained. Forgive me, Mamayya, leave me out of this.

The finality of Kiran's declaration was emboldened by the way he left the hall and moved into his bedroom. Parasuram waited, wondering what else he could do to convince the young man but nothing came to mind.

Finally, with dejection spreading through him like a weight, Parasuram left and returned to Raju who was waiting with the scooter.

*****

Kiran was let with a feeling of the surreal. More than that, what bothered him was that Parasuram might not have given him all the information.

Manipulation, it was.

For Kiran, manipulations, no matter how subtle, don't float past the way people expect them to. Kiran was *smart*, he knew this much for certain himself. While other things were left in the abyss of '*it depends*' or '*there's no way for me to know for sure*', his intelligence had not come into question.

Lies of omission were, in Kiran's opinion, worse than lies told outright. Omission means you're expected to be stupid enough to miss the details, the ones that show there was hidden information in there somewhere.

With each passing minute, he definitely felt he was being manipulated and it only hardened his feelings. He was not going to be a pawn used in their mission that had nothing to do with him.

It didn't. Absolutely nothing.

Besides, why should he be the one to risk his life? Why was his safety something that can be laid on the line for other people? Surely, they'll be able to find someone to fix this? Someone more qualified to exorcise Bhushan's ghos*t?*

Beyond that, what about the reputation he assiduously built on behalf of Kiranmayi? It will go to waste. Especially when they learn that under the veil, under the well-rehearsed and perfectly accurate strains of his body, there was a man. Nobody would come to see him dance.

How could Parasuram expect him to do that?

And what exactly was he going to do to a ghost? He was not a fighter. He had trained only in dance, not martial arts. Definitely not in the art of exorcisms.

What was Parasuram thinking?

Not only that but having to reject the town's Mamayya means that he would be rejected from the town. He had been put in an impossible situation, making him choose between his career, his life and a ghost that he had no place fighting against.

How could *he*, a dancer with the spirit of a female dancer encased inside his soul, be expected to implement Parasuram's plan? What if Parasuram's plan was not as strong as he thinks. What if, as he told Parasuram, he was right, and the ghost kills him? He did not want to die so young, that too in such a violent manner. That's unfair. How can he implement Parasuram's plan?

His parents who now live in the neighbouring state of Tamil Nadu had heard of the killings in the town. They have been asking him to leave the town. At least, take leave from work for a couple of months and come and stay with them, until the murder mystery is solved and the killers caught.

Brushing aside his parent's requests, how can he implement Parasuram's plan?

Maybe taking a break and returning home, away from these issues would be good for him. It would certainly make it difficult for Parasuram to pressurise him into things he cannot possibly do.

Kiran pulled out his phone and called Ravi.

*****

The cold walls reflected the harsh white from the lights that lined the ceiling. Disinfectant stained the air, and Parasuram crinkled his nose against the unpleasant stench. With the beeping, the cries in the distance and urgent calls from doctors, his senses were disturbed in the way they always were when he was in a hospital.

Sravanya lay on starched sheets with her brow creased in pain. Bruises littered her body, IV drips and painkillers sank deep into the skin on her hands, feeding into her veins. Her head and left arm were wrapped in bandages, and her right leg was heavy with a cast, suspended in the air with a sling. Her parents stood on the side of her bed, her father's arms wrapped around her mother who was sobbing into his shoulder.

The curtains blocked out the other residents of the ward, most of whom were awake and talking to their respective visitors.

Just before Parasuram's arrival, Sravanya had listened to a difficult conversation between her parents. One that she likely won't forget but one that she didn't and will never refute, needed to happen. Unfortunately, she hadn't been strong enough to partake verbally.

"I do not understand why she would have gone on such a dangerous mission without telling us first," her mother gasped through tears.

"She must have known that we would have done everything in our power to stop her," her father said.

"And now look at her! Stuck in a bed, hurt and weak."

"She will recover," her father insisted, surely. "Do not grieve for our daughter who will be good as new in a few short weeks."

I have done the right thing, mother and father. I will explain when I am able to, but trust that I made this decision after careful thought and due consideration. The plan was a good one. Everything was in accordance but my physical strength was the only limitation. It let me down more than I have let you down.

Sravanya had spent a long time becoming in-tune with her own body. Such a thing was necessary when your job relies on you knowing and controlling everything your body does, from the way it looks to the way it moves. She had spent years sculpting herself into the model of a perfect dancer. This unbreakable connection had given Sravanya the confidence that adolescence tends to steal away.

Which was why a sudden, unexpected surge of hatred came with a shock of adrenaline.

Her body, which was strong in every sense of the word, was too weak to fight the ghost. Her body had allowed her to become a goddess, given her the ability to dance with magic exuding every motion, and yet she failed.

When Parasuram entered, she pushed herself to wake up fully, much to the loud delight of her parents.

"Why do you brood, Mamayya? You remind me greatly of a wounded lion."

The humour was met with a tight smile.

"I took the challenge wholeheartedly," she assured. "I knew the dangers, and yet I went into it anyway. I do not regret my actions, despite the outcome. I tried. It's all I can ask of myself."

"I shouldn't have asked you," Parasuram said in a low voice.

"You do not believe that I had the strength?"

"I prayed that you would," he explained. "My intentions were for the greater good. I might have miscalculated on our strategy."

Sravanya, despite the dull ache that persisted in her entire body, smiled warmly at Parasuram.

"Do not allow yourself to feel any guilt, Mamayya. And pay no attention to my mother. Her words are as expected. She is a mother, after all. Do they not all speak thus?"

"Indeed they do," he whispered glancing to his left.

"We tried our best. We can ask for nothing more of ourselves than what we were able to give."

Sravanya was alarmed to see the glistening of moistness along the bottom line of his eyelids when Parasuram lifted his head. Nothing leaked down his paler-than-normal cheeks but they were there.

Parasuram was often considered a master of his emotions. Nothing came to surface without his consent, and Sravanya knew that in this moment she was witnessing something no one else in the town had seen.

Parasuram, a majestic, avuncular man, was in a moment of vulnerability and she was blessed with the pain of seeing it. In a split moment, Sravanya had an overwhelming desire to get up, take his hands in hers and put her head on his shoulders as a gesture of comfort. The weight of pain and the shackles of tubes limited her in a way she detested.

Then she said, nay, it felt like a celestial song:

> Killing a demon in dance was entertainment.
> Containing this ghost was *for the greater good*
> It is the ultimate purpose my art and
> I'll never regret my attempt.

A normally reticent lady, who had given her life to mastering her art, considered subduing the ghost as her dance's ultimate purpose and meaning.

The words and the power that they exuded affected everyone in the vicinity.

For Parasuram, they were a zephyr of solace to his inner turmoil. Now he was at peace and it gave room for his mind to start going over the next steps. What were his options?

With Sravanya out of commission, and the ghost still terrorising the town, he needed someone who fits the description of the person needed to rid them of this ghost.

All the while, Ravi was sitting solemnly in a chair. The phone in his pocket vibrated and the word 'Kiran' flashed on the screen.

*****

Kiran held the phone to his ear, foot tapping impatiently on the floor as he waited for Ravi to answer. The conversation with Parasuram had taken its toll mentally.

He'd need to sleep soon, he knew, but when there would be time for that was not something he could discern.

He'd feel better once he had filled a bag with his essentials, ready for his departure.

The other end of the phone crackled, and Ravi's voice came through, crisp and clear. "I hear you refused Mamayya's plan for the ghost?" he said.

Kiran knew the man wasn't really asking but he followed it up with an answer anyway.

"I did."

"I don't blame you," Ravi said with an audible shrug. "I understand, certainly. Any normal person would have said no. Why put yourself in danger when you don't have to, right?"

"And yet you were the one to offer my name, were you not?"

"I was," Ravi said unashamedly.

"And?"

"And what? I could think of no other option, boy. If it were a physical entity, like a rowdy man, I would have taken it upon myself to bash him up, but alas. It's a ghost. Cannot punch a ghost."

Ravi's easy tone and the light way he spoke almost made Kiran want to smile but he didn't. The situation was much darker than the man was letting himself express.

"It's okay," Kiran said eventually. "It's a good thing you're here. I wanted to let you know that I am planning to leave town. Tomorrow. I'll put in the papers and leave by the evening. So, we can say our goodbyes now."

Now Ravi's voice tightened and Kiran sat up straighter, knowing that what he was going to hear would not be good.

"C'mon, don't make such a hasty decision. I do not begrudge your decision to not fight, even for the sake of old friendships. But man, you needn't run."

"It's not running," Kiran muttered, struggling to keep his tone even.

"Come to me. I am at the hospital where Sravanya is admitted. You need not stay long, though I intend to spend the remainder of my evening by her side."

"I don't—"

"We do not need to discuss your decision. If you cannot be swayed to stay, then at least give them your farewell."

Had this been any other time, or any other person, Kiran would have immediately said no. He may not be 'running', but the idea of saying goodbye solidified his intentions. He was not sure he was ready for that.

But this was his best buddy, Ravi. He was relaxed and calm in the conversation and was intent in a way that he could not deny. There was no way that he'd be able to say no to that. Over that, it is courtesy to say farewell.

Kiran was silent for a few seconds. Then he said, "Sure. I guess it's only appropriate that I say goodbye, anyway. I'll be there in thirty minutes."

*****

The bed upon which Sravanya laid was bracketed by Parasuram and Ravi by the time Kiran arrived. The hospital was about twenty minutes from his house. The walk had been short but with the heat of the day, it felt like it had lasted longer.

In fact, knowing what he would have had to do if he were to have engaged immediately made him feel that the rejection he offered was liberating. There was nothing weighing him to a plot he actively decided not to join in with.

Life, for Kiran, was simple. His day job kept a roof over his head and food on his table. All his spare time was given to the practice of dance, perfecting the art he was born to do.

One day, once he'd made enough money to live comfortably, he would marry and settle down, just as society expects. And he's… happy with that plan, he thought. Definitely more so than the one Parasuram put to him. At least his own plan afforded him more years.

Kiran made his way towards the common ward but Ravi spotted him before he walked through the doors. The man jumped up from his seat and came towards Kiran with an intensity that made his stomach twist.

"You weren't joking, were you?" Ravi said, standing up and drawing Kiran from his thoughts. "You truly want to quit your job? I'd hoped that on your way you would have had the time to consider your actions and change your mind."

Shoulders tensing and jumping up to his ears, Kiran glowered.

"Had you warned me this was an ambush, I would have never come!"

Parasuram looked between the bed and the couple talking.

"Mind your volume please," Parasuram warned, eyes hard. "We are in a place of healing."

Kiran grounded his teeth. He breathed deeply in through his nose and let his eyes flicker over the woman in the bed. His body softened in posture and the post-ache from his teeth spread through his gums.

"What was your plan from here, Kiran?" Ravi asked.

"I will live with my parents for a few months," he said, calmly, careful not to cause a scene. "I will find a job in a city such as Hyderabad or Chennai. There are many opportunities in the city that do not exist in this rural town. I've grown sick of the sparsity, and the way my life was open to discussion from strangers. I miss anonymity. Perhaps I will be free to dance as Kiranmayi in the city without concealing my true self."

Ravi sighed. Both walked towards the bed.

There was a tangible guilt in the air that was a struggle to walk through but Kiran refused to take any of it in. It was not his place to feel guilty about something that he had not participated in.

"It was the best decision for me."

Kiran looked towards the bed. It was the first time Kiran saw Sravanya from close quarters. The girl that danced with the grace and skill of a goddess. In adulthood, this woman was a figure on a banner, a name in an advertisement announcing her next event or a dancer on a stage.

And yet a competitor. A force that had ignited ambitions in him. He gazed at her appreciatively: a beautiful diva lying injured on a bed. No one as beautiful as she should be laying prone in a bed after succumbing to injury, mauled by an unrepentant ghost.

Despite the ugliness of her injuries, Sravanya still gleamed with undeniable beauty. The kind that cannot be tainted by bruises or broken bones. No scars could blemish the angelic grace she had been blessed with.

Which begged the question, if she could not tame the ghost, then what business did anyone have expecting him to fare better?

Kiran tried not to cringe under the weight of her look back at him. Her lips parted slightly, and he struggled to understand what it meant. *Was it a half smile or did she intend to say something?*

As he was coming to the end of that thought, a strange sensation came over him.

His body was no longer his own. A trance, though mild, had come over him. He could feel their energies and when their eyes met, he felt a tug of connection. There were people around and in the hall, but in that moment of first eye contact, all identities melted. She and he were two forms of the same persona; they were classical dancers.

They were one.

Kiran had to actively fight it, knowing that he was teetering on the edge of himself.

"I…. I…. came to say goodbye."

And wasn't that ironic, he thought to himself privately. His first words upon meeting this girl were intended to be his last. Not a hello, but a resolute goodbye.

"There are no farewells for the sun."

It was like a spontaneous electric force. Her words struck like lightning, and though he saw her mouth move and the way the others reacted, it was as though she had spoken them directly inside his own head.

The trance was back, stronger now, and emotions flared up inside him that he had no experience with. He had no names for how he felt. Totally caught by surprise, Kiran's trance acquired a halo. A strange emotion he had never felt in his life.

Parasuram understood. Sravanya was urging Kiran to pick up the gauntlet. He moved closer to them.

"I cannot—you cannot truly expect me to fight the ghost," Kiran argued softly, uncertainty tainting his voice.

"It is just a ray of light that dispels darkness. Little does the dark know that the sun is behind the ray."

"This is not my battle," Kiran rebutted weakly.

"What if Lord Ram had uttered those words?" she asked softly. "Imagine that he had refused the battle. Did he?" she waited half a second. "He did not! He fought and rescued Sita."

At this point, Parasuram could not control himself. "Look at her!" Parasuram half-shouted, not minding his own warning from before. "Young man, lay your gaze upon this brave girl. She took up a mighty mission and has shown bravery beyond what anyone expected of her. And do you know what she said, even after defeat? She said humanity's upliftment was the ultimate meaning and purpose of dance."

Kiran looked still at Sravanya, whereas she looked at Parasuram, her eyes imploring him to calm down. Parasuram stood still.

Sravanya continued, "Let the ultimate purpose of dance, *loka kalyanam*, be my perspective. Forget *my* purpose. Shouldn't it be your purpose to leave a legacy?"

Kiran tried his hardest to not react, but even he could not control the twitch on his eyebrow, or the way that his mouth curled around the word 'legacy.'

"Yes, legacy," Sravanya encouraged. "Something that you will always be remembered for. Do you want Kiranmayi to be your only legacy?"

Parasuram butted in again. "Listen to her, Kiran. Do you know that her name, while fit only for a woman, means 'The King of Wisdom'? Grasp the wisdom she offered, young man."

But Kiran didn't want to. He wasn't ready. He never would be.

Against his own wishes, more emotion poured over him and filled him fit to burst. It was one thing listening to the village head's extortions in his room, but another entirely to hear words of a classical dancer. They rang truer, and came from a realm that they both shared. It was like Parvati exhorting Shiva. The influence, the power a woman has on a man!

He became powerless with his decision, but a *shakti* overcame him. His stubborn persistence to deny their wishes started wilting. Sravanya's tired eyes were closing.

"If a Kiran who can drive away darkness, does not do it, who else will?" she whispered. "Do you know who?" Her lips became dry and she closed her eyes.

The room stilled again, the concentrated energy from Sravanya sweeping over him, from afar the whirr of the fan and the electronics around the patients beeping, the surroundings fading off from his consciousness, with another realm beginning to appear, a third eye of wisdom opening up, a man's calling echoed in his heart, engraving itself in his mind, and broken sentences flowed of his mouth as a divine hymn:

> *In the beginning,*
> *in my childhood,*
> *I had lost to you.*
> *Now you lost to a ghost!*
> *O Sravanya,*
> *the king of wisdom,*
> *I will fight,*
> *not for the village.*
> *I will fight,*
> *for myself and for you.*
> *In exorcising the ghost.*
> *Be it death or be it victory*
> *any shall be my legacy.*

Coming back to himself was not unpleasant, but the heavy blanket of fear was lifted, Kiran reached out and clasped his hand around Ravi's.

Turning to meet Parasuram's gaze with the same stubborn certainty he felt before, he said:

"Mamayya, let's do it."

Chapter - 14

Darkness was almost there to pounce upon him, to engulf him. Kiran saw the world in shades of grey but today it was completely black. So much was riding upon him. Everyone's expectations made him hard to breathe as he hiked up the hill alone.

He was not completely alone; Parasuram and Ravi were following him but from a distance. They had decided that Kiran would go in first. Bhushan should not know they were around. Let Bhushan meet the enchanting Kiranmayi. Let *Mohini* cast her spell on the demon. When the demon would be under her spell completely, Kiran would trap the fireflies and Ravi would uproot the shrub.

They didn't carry pots this time, but a steel jar in Ravi's backpack. Ravi had made Kiran conceal a small knife in his dance costume. He did not want to take any chances. They all had learnt their lessons from their previous failure and though Ravi and Kiran both were not a part of the precious attempt, they thought of everything that could go wrong. It was not only their lives but many lives at stake. There was no other option today than winning.

Ravi packed a few tools in his backpack which also gave him confidence. A butcher's knife recently sharpened, two bottles of kerosene, a bunch of matchsticks, two flashlights, and three helmets, not the heavy ones that are used for bikes but like miner's caps, made of leather with frontal glass. He found them on Amazon two days back and ordered a dozen with prime delivery. They arrived this afternoon. He wore leather gumboots and insisted Parasuram also wear them. Only if they had involved Ravi and Kiran before in their plan, Bangaru Babu would have been alive. He sighed!

Kiran stood for a minute, looking up at the sky that was darkening faster. What if he died today? He would be found dead by the police in a girl's costume. And no matter what Parasuram and Ravi explained, it will be in the news that he was Kiranmayi. And what would his father think of him? His father might commit suicide because of the embarrassment. A streak of empathy flitted through him. He took the support of the nearby boulder to steady his breathing. He was in direct face to face with the black fort. And where his hand touched the boulder, a skull was engraved with two cross bones. He wondered who might have drawn that.

The watchers as driver Raju told him that morning when they were planning, "They watch everything and I think they might be telling their master, the ghost in the cave." Of course, paranoia was talking from his mouth. And what kind of people would retain sanity in such circumstances? Very few. People like Sravanya and Parasuram. He was definitely not even the dust of Sravanya's feet. He started walking, thinking of her.

How can someone be so cruel to hurt a beautiful soul like Sravanya. He could not understand. The slow anger that was building up as he thought of Sravanya gave strength to his legs. He kept walking.

What kind of a lover was he? If his love could wage a war against a dark force and get hurt, why couldn't he be brave enough to bring justice to her? He won't allow her pain and suffering to go to waste. She was weak, but she was okay now. A few days of rest and a healthy diet was all that she required. But this black thing, whatever it was, it hurt her. It made her bleed. And he was going to make it pay. He walked in quick stride now closer to the cave.

At that moment, when he was a couple of steps away from entering the cave, his own greyness started to melt. He did not care about the world, about his legacy, about fear, about his father. There was only one thought in his mind - Erase the blackness. And by erasing the blackness he was going to brighten his own greyness, and hopefully his battle with the greyness would finally end. He started to see the enemy within and not outside him. He was about to fight himself. And that was the only way he could win this fight. He was not ambushing some evil entity; he was sparring against a competitor in dance. And let dance be their savior, their leader, and their guide. And let dance be their warfare, too.

Parasuram muttered, "I don't see him."

"He walked too fast as soon as he reached the top." Ravi answered without looking back. He was worried. That idiot could have waited for them. He was supposed to go alone but he was also supposed to maintain a distance from them and not suddenly vanish out of their sight.

"You go Ravi. I will come slowly." Coming back to this place wasn't easy for Parasuram. It was here his son had died. Malati had come back from her trip hearing the news about Bangaru Babu's death. She was inconsolable. She blamed him for not taking care of Bangaru Babu. And she was right. Her words echoed sharply in his ears, *You killed my son.*

When he had lit the fire on his son's pyre, he took an oath to destroy Bhushan. He will not be responsible for any more killings.

This morning, the police cleared him from the murder charges of Bangaru Babu based on the testimony of driver Raju. And also from any serial murder charges. Another murder in the town while he was doing the *puja* for his son's soul at the temple weakened SI Suresh's case. Journalist Subramanyam was also responsible in a way to clear his name. He had vehemently criticised the police department in the *Andhra Velugu* newspaper and pointed out several flaws in the police investigation. He had inferred that the police were trying to wash their hands off by pinning all the murders on the village head, Parasuram, when he was grieving the loss of his foster son. He also mentioned in his article that the case should be transferred to CBI because the local police were not capable of handling a serial killing case. That was a relief, his name cleared from all the murders. But he still had a huge task ahead of him.

He had promised his wife this afternoon that he would either return eradicating the evil spirit or his dead body would return. Malati had hugged him tightly and cried for almost five minutes continuously in his embrace. Those five minutes felt eternal. She had wet his shirt with her tears. She slowly let him go, "I will pray." She ran to the *puja* room and closed the door.

There was also a *mahapuja* that evening in the temple. He could visualise the lights decorating the temple, the whiff of incense scattered in the air, and a serene feeling touching everyone. They needed all the prayers today.

Ravi's words brought him back to the steps of the fort. "I can't leave you alone. It is dangerous. I hope driver Raju could have accompanied us."

"He is safe down there. He has a weak heart. He will not be able to cross these boulders." Ravi nodded and kept walking. He increased his speed, but he also kept looking over his shoulder to keep checking on Parasuram so that he does not lose Parasuram out of his sight. He was not shuddering with fear anymore. His mind was occupied worrying about Kiran, and his body occupied catching up with Kiran's pace. He was satisfied with himself. Last night he thought he would shit his pants and would come trudging down in fear. He felt good about himself.

He caught a glimpse of a lady's back in white *sari* entering the cave. He felt relieved and hurried up to his post. His post was just outside the mouth of the cave. He was meant to watch and at the right time attack or help Kiran. Reaching the mouth of the cave, he removed the two helmets, wore one and gave the other one to Parasuram who also wore it quickly and took his place next to him.

*****

Kiranmayi entered the cave and stood at the mouth of the cave looking at the darkness. She carried a white *jhola* with her. She put it down slowly. She switched on her mobile torchlight and moved it through the cave. She saw two emergency lamps. The police must have left them here when they came for investigation. She switched them on and the darkness swept away.

A shrub stood in her direct eye contact. She felt another man breathing. Though there was no one in the cave she knew someone was watching her. She dabbed lightly on her face with her fingers and with her one hand underneath her chin, she stared at the shrub. She then removed a music player with portable speakers from her bag and hit the play button.

She smiled as the *Guru Stotram* played from the tape. Her audience was the lone shrub.

Guru Brahma, Guru Vishnu,
Guru Devo Maheshwara.

She saluted the shrub in different *Namaskar* poses after the dancer's *Namaskaram*. Pulling her long braid to one side, she stood there watching any movement from the shrub. There wasn't any moment. She played the next song.

Kiranmayi performed all the 108 *Karanas* in this act to the T. In this act a lot of waist and hip movements were embedded. She moved sensuously with her hips swaying beautifully, her legs and hands in perfect sync to her waist movements. Her face radiant like the full moon glowed more brightly than any fireflies. Through the corner of her eye, as she poised briefly, she saw a shadow move.

When she turned and posed again in another *bhangima*[28], she saw the apparition of Bhushan, dressed in a red *sari*. Their hands were in front clasped tightly. They were watching her intently. She smiled at the apparition in a humble bow and continued her dance movements. She was the cosmic beauty; she was of heaven and not of this earth. Bhushan was spellbound with her beauty, grace and her art. They had not seen any dancer dance so beautifully. The perfection that Kiran had achieved as a female dancer made even the trained human eye incapable to discern the difference. The dancer in Bhushan, however, could gauge from the microscopic difference in the elegance of the dance that this was a man dancing. His supernatural instinct confirmed that this was a man.

Rage filled them fast. The apparition was gone now. Kiranmayi stopped her dance wondering what she did to tip off the ghost. She heard a voice, deep and clear like someone was speaking from the far end of a well, "A man!! No reason for a man to be in my cave!! And alive!!"

---

[28] Dance posture.

Their anger started erupting which signalled the fireflies to come for the kill. From afar, Kiran saw the lights approaching.. He had two options: continue with the next dance act to mollify Bhushan or lunge towards the shrub and grab it to suffocate Bhushan. In that moment, Bhushan for all their ghostly powers let out the human instinct of curiosity: *Who are you?*

Kiran realised it was Bhushan's rage that made the shrub glow on and off. The emergency lights burnt off and the glass broke and scattered on the cave's muddy floor. One second, there was complete darkness and in the other second, there was a lustrous glow.

Darkness...red light...darkness again...gold light...darkness...purple light.

Kiran's reflex told him to combine his ideas. Do the dance as well as reach the shrub. Not one or another but both. The voice asked again, "Who are you?"

Kiran went with his gut. He was not standing in front of an enemy, but he was facing a fellow dancer, a brother who had gone astray, a soul engulfed in his own darkness. He should help this unfortunate soul see the light. He opted for a third approach, a split-second decision coming from somewhere from the depth of his heart. Maybe there is a human streak still alive in this ghost.

"I am not a Man. I am not a Woman. I am Shrishti." The word Shrishti reverberated in the cave, Kiran hearing Shrishti in his voice like an echo. He spoke again, "I am very much a child of the universe as you are."

Bhushan became a pupil listening to a sage of wisdom. Still burning under the rage of killing, they managed to say, "You don't know me. The creation you are talking about killed me because I am a transgender. We are not all one." The last lines were so loud that Kiran thought he would be dead with the boomerang effect of the cave that kept echoing even after the voice had stopped speaking.

Ravi and Parasuram impatiently waited outside the cave. They couldn't understand why Kiran was neither dancing nor uprooting the shrub. He was talking in between but he was not supposed to have conversations with the ghost. They decided to go in and pull out the shrub themselves.

Ravi and Parasuram stealthily entered the cave with their bodies pressed against the cave's walls. They stood like statues against the cave's wall. They did not want to startle Bhushan or get caught in their gaze. Slowly, they moved their bodies against the wall until they came around very close to the shrub. They used this opportunity of Kiran engaging Bhushan in a conversation.

Thinking this was the right time, Parasuram bent and reached the shrub and was about to put his hand to pluck it out. From the corner of his eye, Kiran noticed what he was about to do and yelled, "Mamayya, *aagu* (stop)."

Mamayya? The only confidante and friend they had in their life. The only person they could trust more than their parents or anyone else in the village. That was their Mamayya. Who is this Mamayya? Bhushan, the apparition took a look around to see Parasuram and in his persona, his maternal uncle's glimpse for a flicker of a moment came in and went out.

It gave Kiran the opportunity to reply. "You say, the very creation that we are all one, killed you as you were a transgender. But the very creation also gave you an uncle. To you, then. To us, now".

"Don't belittle my Mamayya with this old fox who is trying to kill me again." Bhushan's apparition was back. Their eyes fumed in rage like raw balls of fire. The continuing conversation was a good sign, it meant the parties at fray were willing to listen.

Kiran took a deep breath weighing his words properly, "You were misunderstood, but no longer. I am saying this on behalf of the generations gone and the future ones that are yet to come, you are not them. You are us. You have been killed physically but like you I wanted to be a female dancer, but I was killed emotionally many times. But we will have to find our Mamayyas, our *Mohinis*, our inspirations and continue our journey."

He walked a little further closing the gap between him and Bhushan's apparition, "One of my friends who is a transgender has started to learn *Bharatnatyam* and trust us there won't be another Bhushan in our country. *Meeru cheppandi*, Mamayya (you please tell, uncle).

Parasuram was confused. In their original plan, there were no dialogues for him. They had come here to uproot the evil dwelling in the cave, not for a conversation. But he went along with the plan. He thought for a while and then spoke slowly in a shaking voice, "*Natyanki haddulu levu* (there are no barriers for dancing). Male, female, transgender can dance now. If there is any problem, Mamayya will interfere and solve them." The last lines came out in confidence and were reassuring.

Kiran spoke quickly, "The first *arangetram* (dance debut) of my transgender friend's event is next week and Bhushan will come alive that day on that stage with their performance."

Bhushan was not convinced. All these years of injustice, the torture they suffered at the hands of the rich and powerful could not be forgotten with a few words. "You human beings always go back on your words. You cheat." The apparition pointed a figure at Kiran.

But Kiran was not going to step back, "My life itself is the personification of fight against stereotyping of dancing and stigma against male and transgender dancers. Give trust one chance and show you are better than those people that tortured you. Friend, shall we do one dance together?"

The dance instinct was ignited in Bhushan even with their fiery face. They asked, "Which act?"

"*Nityotsava*[29], the *devadasi* dance that still runs in its glory even after a century." Kiran replied.

*****

In the hospital, Sravanya was anxious. She wanted to go with them but her parents and Parasuram did not allow her.

"Nanna, have they started? Amma, what do you think which colour costume is Kiran wearing? Did they take the helmets? What dance act is Kiran planning? Did he come up with any new one?" Multiple questions. Amma and Nanna both were vexed.

---

[29] Daily Dance Ritual by the devadasis in the temple.

"Don't think too much and stress yourself. You need to rest." Amma scolded Sravanya.

"How can I rest? I want to go," she demanded.

Amma and Nanna tried to convince her that it is dangerous, but she wouldn't listen. Nanna had a slight doubt that she was a little inclined towards Kiran. Did her daughter like him? He decided to ask in a subtle way, "Do you want to help them or are you worried about Kiran?"

"I want to help them…" she fell silent questioning herself. She was worried about Kiran. The image of the shrub attacking her came up in front of her and all that fear and terror she felt made her heart skip a beat. And then the cold body of Bangaru Babu filled her eyes, making them teary.

"I am worried about Kiran too. I just don't want to see him ending like Bangaru Babu." She said, trying her best not to cry. "Nanna, I want to go there. Please take me."

"You are too weak, you can't hike the fort," he said, concerned.

"I will. Please, I beg you."

He could never say no to his daughter. They put her in a wheelchair so that she could use her strength to hike the fort and then they could take her in the wheelchair from the fort to the cave.

They drove up to the fort in their car where driver Raju's minivan was parked at the foot. He did not want to go up there, but if Sravanya could go, he too, could go. All four of them hiked the fort, driver Raju carried the folded wheelchair and a backpack with them.

After they reached the cave, Sravanya was seated at the mouth of the cave. Parasuram and Ravi were inside. She could see the apparition of Bhushan.

Driver Raju asked, "What's happening inside?"

"I don't know. Kiran is saying something about *Nityotsava* Dance," she said.

Driver Raju scratched his head and her parents looked at each other's faces.

*****

Kiran explained to Bhushan, "The *devadasi* who is also called as Nitya Sumangali gives the intent to the ambivalent divinity, giving strength to dispel the evil forces and invite auspiciousness. This is what you wanted to be, and that which you wanted to dispel is what you have become."

At that point of time, the purity of intention made the evil evanescent and the cave sacred like a temple. A *devadasi* rose.

It was their ultimate dream to serve God. And today, they were asked to be a part of that auspicious and holy performance. No one had given them such importance. Their identity itself was ignored. Overwhelmed with emotion, they stepped forward next to Kiran who smiled at them gently.

Their legs beat on the cave's floor, the sound of *ghungroo* reverberated the cave and flowed back to their ears. Their hands moved in unison. They began their dance with waking up the gods with an auspicious beginning. The deities are bathed, clad, fed and decorated. All these acts were performed by the duo followed by *Pushpanjali,* the flower salutation to the Lord. Through *Kumbharti* and other ritual dances, they reenacted the entire *Nityotsava* which starts and ends with the cycle of creation.

They were the Shrishti, they were the *Shakti*, they were the *Purusha*, and they were the *Prakriti*.

As they danced in unison, the fireflies appeared from nowhere dancing with them. The entire cave was sprinkled with golden dust. The fireflies appeared and disappeared as halos around Kiran and Bhushan as they pirouetted and twirled.

Kiran took the lead first and Bhushan followed him. Kiran made a lotus *mudra* and the fireflies sprinkled gold dust on his hand in lotus formation.

He made a movement of waves with his hands and the fireflies formed the waves with their light.

The fireflies blinked and formed different formations doing what Kiran and Bhushan were doing. Everywhere, there was positive energy and vibration.

Bhushan's apparition became golden, fireflies blooming out and in from their form. They filled the cave with streaks of light, splashing gold everywhere. Ravi thought for a moment, there was golden confetti everywhere. The fear from everyone's heart had evaporated by now.

Ravi and Parasuram with their mouths wide open watched this cosmic and sacred dance in awed silence.

Sravanya watching the two stalwarts dancing together felt sheer bliss. Kiran was such a great performer; she did not know. He looked so radiant and beautiful in the white and gold *Bharatanatyam* costume. He looked like a sweet girl. Even though she could not look that beautiful, she thought and smiled.

The fireflies dancing in sync with them made the entire scene heavenly, sprinkling their gold and splashing gold dust everywhere. Lights blinked in varied hues - gold, purple, white - creating a splendid spectrum of a transcendental canvas. They finally reached the last act in their repertoire, singing lullaby for the God and putting him to bed thereby completing one cycle of creation. The day is a metaphor for life and night is the second half, thus a cycle of creation and destruction.

Sravanya was transfixed, witnessing a miracle happening through the mouth of the cave. Sravanya was filled up with a strange joy and happiness seeing Kiran dance in the golden hues of fireflies. Words fell short to describe them. Kiran's dance etched in her memory like Yazaan's song, forever. He was the greatest dancer she had seen till now. Not because of the dance, but the way he spread love in everyone's hearts that day including a century old ghost. Now, she understood her dream. The faceless man who spoke to her, "I have come to teach you the greatest art of all - LOVE."

Her heart was brimming with love. She could not contain the love for Kiran. Oh, how much she wanted to go there, hug him and dance with him.

Raju, and Sravanya's parents tried to adjust themselves by peeping one by one to see what was happening.

Bhushan, while performing the entire *devadasi* dance ritual, understood that their identity did not matter anymore. They were the Shiva and they were the *Shakti*. They were the *Ardhanareeswara* themselves. In their act with Kiran, they assumed the role of Parvati, the goddess, sometimes, and the role of Lord Shiva, sometimes. They were complete. They had offered themselves to God. Their desires were fulfilled. They were liberated. They could not stay anymore.

After they completed the *Namaskaram* marking the completion of their act, Bhushan took Kiran's hands in theirs and shook them in gratitude. Tears of happiness welled from their eyes. Kiran, too, had slayed his darkness. It did not matter anymore whether he was Kiran or Kiranmayi. He himself would announce that he is Kiranmayi in his next performance. His greyness was gone and was replaced by the fireflies' light.

As he smiled at Bhushan, they turned into a million fireflies looking like Bhushan, each firefly moving out of the formation and flying upward. Slowly, they became golden dust and blew away with the wind. The shrub still glowing had grown golden leaves. It started to uproot itself and levitated itself rotating in golden hues. Slowly, it lost its shape and became a big golden bubble dropping to the ground in a loud splash, becoming a puddle of water - colourless and translucent.

The gold dust from Bhushan's apparition settled on the puddle giving it a golden shimmer throughout. It then streamed through the cave. Seeing the stream of water coming out, Sravanya swerved out of its way. The stream travelled through the stones and the boulders seeping into the earth.
Kiran, Parasuram and Ravi rushed out of the cave to see what was happening to Bhushan. The stream became bigger and bigger and as far as their eyes could see, the entire area was lit up with the gold from the water making its way through the boulders and rocks. As it travelled, it sprinkled gold dust on the dried up shrubs and small bushes and the big, dead black tree. It started flowing down through the steps like a golden waterfall from

the slopes of the hill. Bhushan's soul gave an ethereal touch to the entire area.

The gold on the water started to vanish. The water seeped into the earth until the last transcendental streak was absorbed by the earth. It was dark now.

Bhushan's liberation was not only metaphysical but also a moral ascension of the community. Hatred and spite can always be conquered with love. Bhushan did not murder any one today, instead he forgave all the human race. His ascension is also mankind's ascension against bigotry and stigma. Art is neutral. There is no gender in art. Be it a man, woman, or transgender. Anyone and everyone have the right to learn and practise art.

Bhushan left his legacy, the first transgender or many of those transgenders who aspire to be artists but are stalled in their dreams. They never attained lofty heights and remained trapped in the muck of gender discrimination. They simply wanted to be treated equally like any other man or woman.

"This one small step that you took today, Kiran, I don't know how to express myself. We all can't even stand in front of you. You taught a spirit to forgive and taught him love. You gave him *Moksha* (salvation). And we fools were trying to stall it, paralyze it. We did not understand the real essence of life and the vitality of mankind. You opened all our eyes. If I touch your feet also, it will not be enough." Parasuram spoke with tears in his eyes like a child.

"Mamayya, please, you are embarrassing me. I did nothing. We all did it together. I also understood life and love, today." Kiran spoke in a heavy voice. Everyone was emotional.

"I am sorry Kiran. I will never talk about transgenders or other genders cheaply. Neither will I make fun of you or anyone. But when did you change the plan?" Ravi questioned.

"I just went along what my heart said. Bhushan taught me love today. He taught me to accept myself." Kiran could not speak any further.

"Bhushan's libration will become a moral fable for generations to come and it will change people's perceptions. We will tell his story to the world." Parasuram beamed with joy.

"All it took was to treat a transgender equally. His thirst for revenge was quenched and unshackled him from being bound to the earth. And we did not understand that until Kiran showed us that this can be done." Parasuram put his arms, one on Kiran's shoulder and other on Ravi's shoulder and pulled them towards them.

Kiran's eye caught Sravanya on a wheelchair. He almost shouted, "What are you doing here?"

"She made us bring her here. She wouldn't listen. She wanted to know what was happening. She wanted to help you. She threatened us she would cut her nerve if we did not bring her here," Niladri Mullapudi spoke animatedly imitating Sravanya, "We had to bring her here and Raju helped us to carry her up."

Everyone beamed with joy, and all of them started talking at once except Kiran and Sravanya. Kiran squatted so that he could be at eye level contact with Sravanya. No one minded them or observed them as they were all busy talking and celebrating their victory.

"You should be resting. You should not be here. This is dangerous," Kiran said, trying to gauge her expression. Her head was bent.

She slowly lifted her eyes, then her head, "I was worried about you. I could not stay at the hospital." Moonlight on their faces highlighted their expressions and eyes.

Though Kiran was dressed like Kiranmayi, Sravanya only saw Kiran, his eyes were pure and honest.

"Did you see me dance?" He asked.

"Yes. The whole act." There were tears in her eyes.

"Why are you crying? Did I do something wrong?"

"No. You were superb. You were great. I could not have performed like you." She sniffled, controlled her tears, she wanted to talk more but she could not.

She was brimming with love and to tell what all she felt in the last one hour was difficult to explain. Her jinx of a 10 year period was broken. She had found love. She was having the same emotion she had when she was listening to Yazaan's song on a bench near the Hudson river and the seagulls flying over them.

She could not contain her love for Kiran. She wanted to tell Kiran how she felt but words could not describe her emotion. She leaned forward and kissed Kiran on his lips.

Kiran was shocked. And then he grinned. Sravanya blushed. Words were not necessary at all. He understood what she felt for him. He felt the same for her for a long time.

Suddenly, the earth trembled. They felt tremors under their feet. They rushed to hike down. And when they were safe down at the foot of the hills, Raju squealed in happiness pointing at the fort, "Look, the watchers are gone." They all dismissed his words and came back to town in the minivan and the car.

There was a swish of fireflies on the *kacha* road behind them as they drove towards the light, into the dawn.

* * * * *

About the Author: Kalam Babu

Kalam Babu is a senior software professional who enjoys natural language processing, both the machine learning and non-machine-learning types. In real life as well as in literary pursuits, he values simplicity.

A graduate of VNIT Nagpur, he has an MBA from Webster University (USA), and takes delight in being a reader, programmer, writer and manager. Kalam Babu founded HydRAW in 2018. He reads and writes across a wide variety of genres and themes.

Kalam Babu has published three short-story collections: *It Did Not Happen One Night* (2018), *There Is No One New Around You* (2019) and *Transition* (2020).

His short story *The Questionnaire* was published in HydRAW's anthology *Advent*.

About the Author: Lavanya Nukavarapu

 Lavanya Nukavarapu is a finance professional who used to deliberate only on finance until one day poems and stories beckoned her. She became a compulsive writer who could not go to sleep without penning at least a few words every day. Her first book *Bare Thoughts*, a collection of her poems was published in 2018. In 2019, Lavanya published her first novel, *The Captive*, a psychological thriller that has received outstanding reviews. Her second novel *Cigarettes Sex Love* published in 2020 explores the complexities of modern-day relationships.

A research paper on Bare Thoughts, The 21st Century Perspectives in the Poems by Lavanya Nukavarapu was presented in February, 2020 by Prof. Saumalya Mali of Saldiha College, Bankura (W.B.) at the seminar "Recent Trends in Indian Women's Literature" organised by Midnapore College, Midnapore, West Bengal.

If metaphors and imagery are the mojos in her poetry, it is narration in her prose, manifested in the several short stories and poems published in various journals and platforms. Lavanya won the 52 weeks story telling competition, 2018 conducted by StoryMirror. She is also a professional editor and likes to help upcoming authors in editing/guiding their works and promoting new talent. Her prior editing works include a historical fiction novel, a self-help and a political thriller.

Her social media handle is Lavanya Nukavarapu.

About the Editor: Dr Rizia Begum Laskar

A gold medalist in M.A. in English, 2003 from Tezpur University, Dr. Rizia Begum Laskar is a teacher by profession with a doctorate degree in children's literature. She has been teaching for the last 12 years in a college in Dibrugarh, Assam.

She got her Ph.D. from Tezpur University in January, 2016 on the topic *Negotiating Home in Indian English Children's Literature: A Study of the Selected Works of Ruskin Bond, Arup Kumar Dutta, Anita Desai, Shashi Deshpande and Salman Rushdie.*

Rizia's primary interests lie in reading rather than in writing. She has been associated with editing a few books which are basically subject related. She has also published academic articles in an array of books and journals. She is also the life member of Council for Teachers' Education, Assam Chapter.

About Sohini Roychowdhury (who wrote the foreword)

Sohini Roychowdhury, Indian dancer, choreographer, visionary, philosopher and professor of Natyashastra, is the founder of Sohinimoksha World Dance & Communications and Sohinimoksha Artes de La India in Madrid, Kolkata and Berlin. Sohini and her multinational Sohinimoksha troupe´s world-view, and mission, is Connecting Civilizations, and enriching lives, through art, music and dance. A premier ambassador of Indian culture for the last several years, Sohini´s performances – solo and with her multinational troupe, have been garnering tumultuous audience appreciation, and rave critical reviews all over the world.

Groomed under the classical Tanjore style, Sohini combines the best of two worlds - a classical conservative training and a modern innovative outlook. Her dedication and special talent as an exponent of India's oldest classical dance, Bharatanatyam, her unique choreography and stagecraft, her ability to adapt and fuse the best that the world of International dance and music has to offer with her Bharatanatyam based choreographies, her culture and language bridging communication skills, have all combined together to create the unique world of Sohinimoksha.

A regular speaker on Natyashastra, Dance, Gender Empowerment, Motivation through the Arts and related topics, Sohini is a visiting Professor at a number of Universities and institutes in Europe, the Americas and India.

Sohini is a winner of the "Mahatma Gandhi Pravasi Samman" by The House of Lords, British Parliament; the Priyadarshini Award for Outstanding Achievement in Arts, New Delhi; Exceptional Women of Excellence Award by the Women Economic Forum, New Delhi and has been a European Brand Ambassador for India Tourism´s "Incredible India" campaign.

Sohini has been called "a revolutionary in the world of music and dance" by the Hindustan Times and "remaking history in the footsteps of Uday Shankar" by the Times of India.

Born in a family of illustrious musicians and artists, in Kolkata, India, Sohini took up training in Indian classical dancing, at the tender age of eight, under Thankamani Kutty and Guru Venkitt, renowned and respected gurus of Bharatanatyam and Mohiniattiam.

About Uma Makala
(who did the front cover painting)

Coming from a family of poets and writers, Uma Makala, had an urge to write and a passion for storytelling. Life's proclivity led her to a different medium, that of 'colours and canvas', where she spreads her thoughts and emotions.

Uma paints to express herself and her subjects are mostly women and nature in harmony and bliss. Her art works have been exhibited in the galleries of Hyderabad and other cities. She lives in Hyderabad with her husband Venu Gopal and their lovely daughter and son.

9 788194 916413